A TEXAS-MADE FAMILY

BY
ROZ DENNY FOX

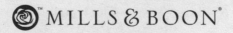
MILLS & BOON

First published in Great Britain 2010
Harlequin Mills & Boon Limited,
Eton House, 18-24 Paradise Road, Richmond, Surrey TW9 1SR

ISBN: 978 0 263 87951 3

23-0210

Harlequin Mills & Boon policy is to use papers that are natural, renewable and recyclable products and made from wood grown in sustainable forests. The logging and manufacturing processes conform to the legal environmental regulations of the country of origin.

Printed and bound in Spain
by Litografia Rosés S.A., Barcelona

"Can we meet on Friday?"

Grant asked, as he pulled a business card out of his pocket and jotted down his number. "Same time as today and same place."

"How about one o'clock? Why don't I bring an extra sandwich for you?" Rebecca was beginning to warm to the idea of seeing him again.

"No. Let me bring the food. My daughter's so sure I can't even boil water, I need to prove I'm not a total kitchen klutz."

Rebecca's laughter welled up from deep inside and brought colour to her cheeks. "All right, but you've got to promise we'll come up with some kind of plan for the kids. Otherwise I can't justify meeting you for lunch."

That dampened his spirits a bit. "I promise," he murmured. "Between now and Friday, I'll figure out how to make peace with Ryan. I should be able to relate to him better."

"I hope so. Our kids are the whole reason for us to see each other. Bye, Grant." She hurried into the salon where she worked.

As he called out a final goodbye and headed for his car, Grant thought he should have corrected Rebe_____ he want___

Available in February 2010
from Mills & Boon®
Special Moments™

Roz Denny Fox has been a RITA® Award finalist and has placed in a number of other contests; her books have also appeared on the Waldenbooks bestseller list. She's happy to have received her twenty-five-book pin and would one day love to get the pin for fifty books. Roz currently resides in Tucson, Arizona, with her husband, Denny. They have two daughters.

CHAPTER ONE

REBECCA GEROUX barely made it to the kitchen with her three heavy bags of groceries before one ripped open. Oranges spilled across the counter. Two bounced off and hit the floor. "Lisa!" Rebecca called for her sixteen-year-old-daughter, hoping for some help.

Getting no answer, Rebecca tried her son. "Jordan! Hey, one of you kids had better get in here, or I won't have time to fix supper before I need to leave." From the silence that ensued, she knew Jordan hadn't heard. That wasn't surprising—he'd had his nose in a book and music blaring from his new iPod as she passed him on the couch. Rebecca didn't see the appeal of an iPod, but all kids lately seemed to need one. And Jordan had done odd jobs to earn the money for his. Rebecca just hoped the book in his hand was homework.

Gathering up the errant oranges, she dumped them in a fridge drawer. *Thank goodness I can multitask,* she thought as she stacked canned vegetables on an upper pantry shelf while she filled a large pot with water to boil for spaghetti. Finding a jar of commercial tomato sauce tucked behind the beans, she wrenched it open and poured it into a smaller pan.

Being a single mom who'd worked two jobs for what seemed like forever, Rebecca had long since stopped beating herself up over using shortcuts. She did whatever it took to keep a roof over her family's heads and food on the table. Not to mention clothes on the body of a teenage boy who grew an inch a month.

It was lucky Lisa waited tables a couple of afternoons a week and the occasional weekend. She babysat, too, for Darcy Blackburn, one of Rebecca's co-workers at the restaurant. It wasn't easy, but every penny helped build the college fund Lisa and Rebecca contributed to every week. Lisa was going places. With her straight A's and work ethic, she was never going to be stuck working two jobs.

"Lisa!" Rebecca yelled again. "Come take over the dinner. I've got to change before I leave for the Tumbleweed. At the salon today, I dribbled a big splotch of red hair dye down my blouse. I can't serve customers like this."

The side door crashed open, catching Rebecca so off guard she dropped the loaf of French bread she'd just buttered and wrapped in foil.

"For heaven's sake, Lisa Louise, you scared the living daylights out of me. I thought you were in your room doing homework. Where have you been?"

The pretty blond girl shed her backpack. "Sorry, Mom. I told Jordan to let you know I was taking the late bus home today." Lisa washed her hands at the sink, then leaned over the stove to peer into the pots. "Spaghetti again?" She wrinkled her nose. "Did you read the article I brought home from health class? Eating all these starchy foods is *so* fattening."

Rebecca smoothed a hand down her worn black slacks. "Then it's a good thing this family burns calories off with hard work." Handing Lisa a wooden fork, she added dryly, "If you feel the need for extra exercise, you can dance while you stir. Just keep the noodles from sticking. Oh, and don't put anything down the garbage disposal. It quit again. There goes another hundred bucks." Rebecca heaved a sigh.

Reaching back into the pantry, she made room for several giant cereal boxes. "So…why *did* you take the late bus home?"

"We got a new student. Mom, he is totally hot. Ryan Lane. He's a senior. Actually, he's been in town a few weeks, but couldn't start class until the records from his previous school arrived. He's in my honors English and honors chemistry classes. Mr. Reavis made Ryan my chemistry partner. Ever since Ginny Parker's dad got transferred to an airbase in Maryland I've been the only one doing experiments alone."

Rebecca shut the cupboard and frowned. Her mind had stalled on the *totally hot* comment. "So, did Mr. Reavis ask you to stay after class to share your notes with the new boy?"

But Lisa wasn't listening. "Ryan plays baseball.

He's a pitcher. Coach asked him to try out for the team, and Ryan invited me to watch. Mom, he's nothing like the other jocks. Ryan's been going to school in Germany for years. And he has the coolest convertible ever. Baby blue. The exact shade of his eyes," she murmured, oblivious to the fact that her vigorous stirring had slopped water out of the noodle pot.

"You can't afford to be distracted by boys, Lisa," Rebecca chided. "If you expect to get one of these scholarships we researched, you have to keep your grades up and stay in the honors programs. Surely I don't need to remind you how long it took me to save up for beauty school? And even after I passed the course I couldn't afford to rent space in a shop right away because I needed all the hours I could get at the Tumbleweed just to pay the bills."

The girl made a face. "Yeah, yeah. Like you'd ever let me forget. You *asked* me why I was late, so I'm explaining."

"I know. I'm trying to be clear about why you can't lose sight of your goal of going to a really good college."

"Right. But, Mom, you've got to meet Ryan. He's smart. And nice."

"Nice is as nice does, young lady. What about his parents? What do you know about them?"

"I think it's only him, a little sister and his dad. But when I bragged about what a great mom you are, Ryan said he'd like to meet you."

"Monkey! You think you'll distract me with flattery? Just remember what I said, okay?" Rolling her eyes, Rebecca began ticking off the chores that Lisa and her brother needed to take care of while she was gone. "Darn, I still have to change this blouse. I'll get Jordan to set the table." Rebecca ruffled Lisa's hair as she left the kitchen.

She had good kids, she reminded herself as she detoured to the laundry room to rub spot cleaner into the stain on her white blouse. She wished she and Lisa could have a more easygoing relationship. But the responsibility for the family's well-being was all Rebecca's. Their household ran as smoothly as it did thanks to the rules she'd implemented. One she always insisted on—eating at least two meals a day together in spite of her crazy work schedule. Tossing the blouse in with the rest of the laundry, she prayed it'd come clean as she set the load to wash, and hurried off to find something else to put on.

When everyone was finally seated around the table, Rebecca pumped Jordan about how *his* classes were going. Lisa didn't voluntarily mention hers. When pressed, she said, "I'm researching an interesting English paper on early women authors. Did you know some had to use male pseudonyms in order to get published?"

Rebecca listened intently. "Life hasn't been a walk in the park for women in a lot of fields, Lisa."

Finishing her meal first, Rebecca rose and rinsed

her plate in the sink. "Don't forget, kids. No using the disposal until I get someone to check it out."

"When will that be?" Lisa asked. "It smells yucky, too."

"It won't be until I can find room in the budget," Rebecca said, collecting her purse and dropping a quick kiss on each child's head. "Lock up," she cautioned out of habit. "I close the restaurant all week, so leave a light on. And, Jordan, no staying up to watch late shows."

"Mom, we know all that stuff," Lisa said. "We're not babies anymore."

"Humor me, okay? Old habits are tough for old moms to break."

"You always say that. Forty isn't old," Lisa said testily. "Age is a state of mind."

"Well, then I must be ancient," Rebecca shot back right before she went out and shut the door.

Her car coughed and died, coughed and died again. At last she coaxed the engine to turn over. Once out on the street, she patted the dashboard. Her car wasn't getting any younger, either. Every day Rebecca battled San Antonio's rush-hour traffic as she dashed between two jobs and home. Tonight was no different, but at least she was relatively satisfied that she had her household back on track. Lisa hadn't mentioned the new boy again. Hallelujah! At least *that* problem had been successfully nipped in the bud.

REBECCA CONTINUED with that assumption through three idyllic weeks, during which things ran smoothly at the salon, at the restaurant and at home.

On Monday afternoon of the fourth week, however, she got home late because of more car trouble. She rushed into the house, out of sorts from having to wait for the bus after an unsettling call from Lisa's school counselor. Giving Jordan's foot a shake as she passed him on the couch, Rebecca said, "The Nissan's kaput. When I left the salon, it refused to start and I had to have it towed to a repair shop. I'm running really behind. Jordan, are you listening? Get Lisa. I need a private word with her, and then the two of you throw together BLT sandwiches for supper. There's lettuce and tomato in the fridge. Fix bacon in the microwave. That's all we have time for tonight, I'm afraid."

"Lisa's not home yet. She stayed for the baseball game. Ryan's the opening pitcher. He said he'd drive her home after the game."

Rebecca skidded to a halt on the way to her bedroom. "Run that by me again."

Unfolding his long body from the too-short couch, Jordan peered at his watch. "Lisa thought she'd beat you home. Usually she does. Today's game must've gone into extra innings."

"Are you saying this isn't the first time your sister's stayed after school for a baseball game?"

"Yeah. She watches the home varsity games.

She'd like to sign up for the rooter bus, but she thinks you'd have a fit."

"That explains why her counselor called me at work. She's concerned about a sudden slip in Lisa's grades. Listen, Jordan, I need to take a quick shower. Then you and I will walk over to the school. I haven't got a clue where the ball diamond is. You can show me."

"Aw, Mom. What's the big deal? Lisa's a brainiac. What's the harm if she goofs off a bit?" Jordan's question was drowned out by the slam of his mother's bedroom door.

Following a very short shower indeed, Rebecca rushed back to the living room. Her coral-colored hair was darker than normal because she'd skipped drying it. She ignored the water spots on the light blue blouse she was tucking into a navy twill skirt.

Jordan launched a second argument against walking to the high school. "It's a dumb idea, Mom," he said, "Ryan could take a different route home and miss us alto—" He broke off when a key rattled in the lock and the door opened. Jordan raised a warning eyebrow at his sister, who was completely absorbed in something her companion was saying.

The boy trailing Lisa into the house towered over her by more than a head. He wore a dirt-streaked ball uniform and his nut-brown hair had a wind-blown, precision cut. No run-of-the-mill barber-shop cut, Rebecca noted. But it was the kid's possessive hand on her daughter's waist that sent Rebecca's mind reeling.

"Oh, hi, Mom," Lisa said belatedly. "I didn't see your car. I…uh, didn't think you were home." Grabbing her new friend's hand, Lisa dragged him fully into the room. "Ryan's game ran late. He won it with his brilliant pitching." Lisa sent him a dazzling smile. "The coach let Ryan pitch the whole game. And he struck out the last three batters. Ryan, this is my mother, Rebecca Geroux. Mom, Ryan Lane, Central High's pitching star." Lisa didn't bother to hide how enamored she was of the boy, who appeared to accept her admiration as his due.

Lisa babbled on, unaware of her mother's growing tension. "I happened to mention to Ryan that our garbage disposal quit and is starting to smell really gross, Mom. He said he installed one in their house in Germany. He's offered to look at ours to see if it's worth fixing, or if we need to replace it. Either way, his labor's free."

Ryan held out his hand to Rebecca. "Happy to finally meet you, Mrs. Geroux. Lisa's told me a lot of nice things about you." His smile and the way he knew all the right things to say felt calculated to Rebecca. He seemed far too carefree to suit her.

Oh, yes, the counselor's phone call suddenly made perfect sense. Lisa looked at the kid as if he made the sun rise and set. Ryan Lane was to blame for Lisa's inattention to her schoolwork.

Rebecca had once married a boy with an engaging

smile and a sense of entitlement. She had no intention of allowing Lisa to fall into the same trap.

Closing her eyes briefly, Rebecca dug deep to ground herself in the present. She didn't want to remember the day she'd been forced to flee from Jack Geroux and find safety for herself and Lisa in a shelter. She'd learned the hard way that smiles and empty promises spelled disaster for a girl with no money of her own and far too little education.

When Rebecca opened her eyes again, all she could see was Ryan Lane's arrogance. She couldn't bring herself to shake his hand. For Lisa's sake, Rebecca wanted this boy—Ryan—to disappear.

"Mom?" Lisa gripped Ryan's left arm, but she'd begun to gnaw her lip in consternation at her mother's silence.

Rallying at last, Rebecca found her voice and steeled herself. She abruptly stepped between them, effectively separating Lisa from the cocky interloper. "Excuse me, you'll have to go. I need to leave for work, and with you bringing Lisa home so late our evening routine has been disrupted. While we're on the subject of my daughter, let me be perfectly clear. She can't afford to be distracted from her studies by hanging out at baseball games. As for our disposal, thanks for the offer, but I've called a plumber."

She hadn't, of course, and both her kids knew it.

Even though Ryan Lane was taller and broader than Rebecca's five foot four and one hundred and twenty pounds, she edged him out the door. Her final glimpse of him showed the smile had been wiped off his face as he gaped at her from the bottom step.

Rebecca shut the door before she had to give any explanation for her rudeness.

Lisa promptly burst into tears. "*Mother!* How could you embarrass me like that? I'm not a child. I'm almost seventeen. I hate you! I'm never going to speak to you again. I wish I knew where Daddy was so I could go live with him. He wouldn't be so mean to me." Flinging her backpack to the floor, she ran down the hall to her bedroom.

Rebecca slowly released her hold on the door-knob. She clasped her hands together to keep them from shaking. Why in the world would Lisa say such a thing about her father? They never mentioned him. He had no place in any of their lives.

Avoiding her son's look of dismay, Rebecca picked up Lisa's pack and set it on the couch.

Jordan flopped down beside the well-used pack. "Boy, remind me never to bring a girlfriend home."

"Ryan is *not* Lisa's boyfriend."

"Huh! That's what her friends at school call him. The other girls are jealous. Anyway…what's wrong with her having a boyfriend? It's no big deal, Mom. You act like dating is a capital offense."

"Dating? Have they been seeing each other at more than those silly baseball games?" Rebecca crossed to the window and tugged aside the drape.

A pristine blue Mustang convertible was parked at the curb. Ryan Lane stood beside it with his car keys in his hand, facing the house, chin defiantly elevated. He scowled one final time, before slowly stepping off the curb to climb into his fancy car. With a roar, he drove away.

What a contrast to her own battered compact, which now languished in a repair shop until she could find the money to bail it out. And didn't the age and condition of the cars alone underscore the vast difference between that boy's family and Lisa's?

Rebecca let the drape slide through her fingers. She paused as she remembered what else Lisa had said about Ryan's family—that he didn't have a mother. It was possible that his father—another single parent—might not be any happier than she was about his son pursuing a girl.

Moreover if the family was as well off as that convertible implied, Rebecca doubted very much that Mr. Lane would be thrilled with her own situation. "Jordan, do you happen to know Ryan's father's first name?" If she had that, Rebecca could phone the man and maybe enlist his help in nipping the fledgling relationship in the bud.

"Nope. Maybe Lisa knows. So, Mom, are we still gonna eat before you head out, or what?" Jordan asked, eyeing his mother uneasily. "Aren't you late already?" The fourteen-year-old picked at a frayed sofa cushion before slapping both knees and standing up.

"Guess there's nothing stopping me from making BLTs," he said.

"I can't leave like this. I'll phone Darcy and see if she'll cover my shift." All at once, Rebecca felt guilty for the way she'd handled things. She should've thought about contacting the boy's father instead of losing her temper. She could have politely sent Ryan away and then sat down with Lisa to discuss her school counselor's call. They still needed to do that. When Lisa was calmer, she'd see what hanging out with Ryan was doing to everything she'd accomplished so far. And if she didn't—then Rebecca could involve Ryan's father.

"Fix yourself a sandwich if you want, Jordan. I'm not hungry. I doubt Lisa will be, either."

"I'm sorry, Mom."

"Jordan, none of this is your fault."

"Lisa's in deep shit, huh? Are you gonna ground her forever?"

"Jordan, watch your language, please. I…uh… will handle Lisa."

"You better not try now, Mom. She's too upset to hear anything," Jordan said sagely. "You might wanna wait awhile, so why don't you just go to work?"

"Maybe you're right." Truthfully, giving up a shift would cost money Rebecca desperately needed to pay for the repairs to the Nissan and the smelly garbage disposal that no amount of disinfectant seemed to help. The kids had no idea how tight their finances were each month. Any unexpected expense meant cutting back someplace else. Subtract a night's wages and tips and, well, she had no way to cut the budget that much.

"I really should go in to work tonight," she said to her son, still waffling.

"Yeah, the restaurant's always busy. Mrs. Blackburn might have trouble handling your tables and hers."

"I'd better phone Darcy anyway, and let her know I'll be late. I'll offer to close for her tonight if she'll cover my tables until I can get downtown." Rebecca's co-worker, Darcy Blackburn, was also a single mom with four young boys. She, too, had trouble making ends meet and would understand kid trouble without asking a bunch of questions Rebecca wasn't prepared to answer.

After talking to Darcy, Rebecca knocked softly on Lisa's door. The crying didn't lessen, so she tried the knob. She wasn't surprised to find the door locked. "Lisa, open up. We need to talk before I go to work."

"No. Just because *you* hate men doesn't mean I have to. You ruined my life. Go away."

Rebecca took a breath to respond, then let it out on a sigh. Jordan was right. Lisa wouldn't listen when she was in this frame of mind. How could she make her daughter, who'd never experienced real hardship, see that a woman needed a good education in case she had to support herself?

Yes, Rebecca's marriage had fallen apart, but she didn't hate men. She just didn't have time for a relationship. She'd assumed that her kids would look at her as an example and avoid repeating her mistakes.

Leaning her head against the door, she said, "Jordan's fixing BLTs. I'm leaving for the restaurant. When I get home, we'll discuss this further, Lisa."

"No, we won't! You were rude to Ryan. Now he'll never speak to me again."

"Listen up, kiddo. We have rules about schoolwork being a priority. You broke them big-time. Are you aware that your counselor phoned me to say you haven't handed in some vital assignments, and you've slipped from an A to a C in two classes?"

"I don't care!" The sobbing intensified. It hurt to hear how broken-hearted her daughter sounded. Rebecca was torn between calling Darcy back and canceling work tonight, or digging deeper and simply attending to duty.

Just as it had been ever since her divorce fifteen years ago, duty won. Turning away from Lisa's door, Rebecca pulled a sweater from her closet and ran a brush through her tangled hair.

"Jordan," she called from the front door. "I'll do my best to catch the eleven-twenty bus. I hope I'll be home by midnight."

Her son stepped out of the kitchen, sandwich in hand. "I wish you only had to work at the beauty shop, Mom. Me and Lisa never get to hang with friends. Like Lisa said, we aren't babies anymore. I don't understand why you won't trust us."

"I trust you, Jordan. Honey, I work two jobs so that your future, and Lisa's, will be secure. Be better than mine. You'll have plenty of time after you get your education to hang out with friends."

"Maybe we'd rather have a little fun now." His eyes remained darkly accusatory as he bit into his sandwich.

Rebecca had the door open, and she saw her bus lumbering through the intersection, so she had to leave immediately or put Darcy in a bind.

She hated to go feeling as if she'd failed both her kids. All of this unhappiness had come about in a matter of weeks. Because of that boy—Ryan Lane.

Maybe Darcy could help her decide whether to contact the boy's father.

Running to catch her bus, Rebecca was out of breath when she climbed on and took the first available window seat. The bus was nearly empty, so Rebecca had a seat by herself. The long ride, unfortunately, allowed her too much time to think.

Had she been wrong to hide so much of her past from her children? They knew she'd grown up in a Mennonite community in Oregon's Willamette Valley. Once or twice she'd probably mentioned working from dawn to dark in the community orchards and in the sheds, stirring hot vats of apple butter and peach preserves. Maybe she hadn't been clear enough that leaving the order and her family had had nothing to do with the work, but with the highly restrictive lifestyle. That was why she'd married Jack. They'd both wanted out.

Lisa and Jordan knew she'd been estranged from her folks since before they were born. They seemed to accept the lack of grandparents, so Rebecca had never felt a need to explain the practice of shunning.

But even prior to the shunning, Rebecca had always felt stifled in the small community. She had routinely spent hours in a barren chapel kneeling on hard wooden planks. Her parents, the Epps, did shop occasionally in the nearby town. It was on those outings that Rebecca glimpsed how other people lived. People not bound by austere beliefs.

By the time she was in high school, many of her friends had quit school to work on the family farm. Very few attended the secular public school in Salem.

Families in her community were split between Mennonite and a more rigid sect—the Amish branch of the Anabaptist-Mennonites. The Amish eschewed all modern conveniences and traveled by horse and buggy. Rebecca's family, being just as spiritually focused but slightly less culturally separatist, allowed her to ride the school bus that stopped at the bottom of their hill.

Her first day of high school, she'd shared a seat with Lacy Hoerner, another freshman, who turned out to be a font of information. Rebecca had been like a sponge. Every day her book bag held a sandwich, an apple and a Bible. Lacy's was more like a portable cosmetic counter, full of lipstick, eye shadow, mascara and nail polish in every color of the rainbow. As well, Lacy was a master at conjuring up all the latest hairstyles. Rebecca liked being her model and, right then, longed to be a beautician one day. That was the most enjoyable period of her life. Then her brother, Mark, two years older and far more aligned with the church's teachings, tattled to their parents and ruined everything.

Her parents came down on her hard. It was the end of her schooling in town. The end of all future trips there. She had tried to give up wanting to learn, tried to go home and be the dutiful Mennonite daughter. But she wasn't able to do it. That small taste of the outside world led to a series of decisions that seemed right at the time, but eventually proved to be a big mistake. Even so, she'd relive even the worst years to be able to have her children.

That was why it had felt like a knife in her heart when Lisa announced today that she wished she could go live with her father.

The bus slowed, jerking Rebecca out of her memories. She looked out the window and saw she'd arrived at the stop a block from the Tumbleweed. She thanked the driver as she swung down. Walking the block blew the cobwebs of the past from her mind.

Rebecca was in the kitchen, tying on her apron, when one realization became very clear. No, she couldn't roll back time, but she could try to keep

Lisa from messing up her life. "I'm going to contact Ryan Lane's dad," she muttered.

"Uh-oh. Talking to yourself is a bad sign," Darcy Blackburn said in a cheery voice from right behind Rebecca.

Startled, Rebecca smacked her elbow on the wall. "Jeez, Darcy, don't sneak up on me like that."

The lanky blonde shifted two plates of steaming meatloaf. "Honey, a six-foot woman in a size-ten shoe never sneaks anywhere. Are you okay?" she added. "You've been frowning since you walked in."

"It's Lisa. She's been goofing off, skipping study time to hang with a boy. A baseball player of all things."

"Haven't we taught that girl anything?" Darcy rolled her eyes. "Well, you don't complain about your ex so much. But Lisa's heard me fighting with Kevin over child support more than once. I'm certainly not one to hold back how I feel about living two steps from welfare because I stupidly left high school to marry Mr. Wrong."

"True. Hey, you'd better deliver those plates before they go cold. Maybe we can catch a minute later to talk. I could use some advice before I dive into the next dreaded mother-daughter chat."

"Glad I have four boys. I expect I *will* go through the terrible teens, but I figure I'll muddle through. Apparently it's against the law to lock 'em in a closet until they gain some sense."

"Darcy!"

"Just kidding," she called and sped off to her customers.

Sure, Darcy could joke. But just wait until one of her boys did something to break her heart. As Rebecca picked up meals from the cook and delivered them, she thought how vociferously Darcy insisted she'd never get married again. Rebecca hadn't ruled out the possibility, but she never had time to meet anyone.

Work kept her from focusing on her personal problems for the rest of her shift. The Tumbleweed's proximity to the River Walk meant they had a steady stream of customers. The two friends never found time to chat. At ten-thirty, Rebecca balanced the till, then helped Darcy set up tables for the breakfast crowd.

"I'd offer you a lift home," Darcy said, "but my mom has the boys. I only use her in emergencies, and they're too rambunctious for her to handle over a long evening."

"What happened to your new sitter? Lisa said she seemed great."

"Yeah, well, turned out she was pregnant. Her folks pressured her to go back to the jerk for the sake of the baby." Darcy made a sour face. "Been there, done that. I told her all that got me was the twins. I predict she'll learn that it takes more than a baby to save a bad marriage. Why is it so difficult to find a reliable sitter? Constant turnover is hard on my boys."

"Why not ask Lisa to fill in? That could solve my problem temporarily. If you make it clear she's not to have friends over, maybe it would discourage this boyfriend thing."

"You think this kid will dump Lisa if she stops mooning over him at his baseball games? Wouldn't surprise me. Men want all the attention focused on them."

"Well, Lisa needs college money. And she loves sitting for your boys."

"I'll phone her when I get home. Do you think she'll still be awake? And what about her shifts here?"

"I'm sure Max will work around your schedule. Lisa plans to be an elementary school teacher. She loves doing creative stuff with your boys."

"So do I. Unfortunately I'm usually too tired. Everything falls on me since Kevin sailed off into the sunset with his most recent bimbo. Honestly, how can I expect the boys to grow up when their dad hasn't? You haven't heard the latest. She's barely out of her teens, but she has boobs out to here." Darcy cupped her hands away from her chest. She was still built like the runner she'd been when she first married Kevin. "Come let me out. It upsets me to talk about Kevin. He'll never change."

Rebecca lingered at the door. "It's not fair that you have to work two jobs to provide for his boys, and he gets to squander his money on a yacht to impress other women. Have you talked to your lawyer about upping his support?"

"She tells me boats are intangible assets." Darcy grimaced.

"You mean if I sell my house and buy a boat my kids will qualify for college grants?"

"Raising kids on a boat isn't practical. And you do everything possible to give your kids a nice, normal life."

And that, Rebecca decided after Darcy left, was the bottom line—even if Lisa suddenly didn't agree.

Which she didn't. When Rebecca wearily dragged herself in on the dot of midnight, Lisa was still angry.

"It's late and we're both tired, kiddo. All I'm going to say is that I consider it important that we eat together as a family. You let us down today, not to mention blowing off family time to attend an athletic event I knew nothing about."

"I didn't tell you," Lisa said, slamming her pencil down on the kitchen table, "because I wanted to avoid this argument. It's not Ryan's fault you and Daddy had a horrid marriage. You are just so biased against men."

"I am not. Why would you say that?"

"I wonder." Lisa pursed her lips. "Do you think Jordan and I don't hear you and Darcy bashing men? Well, mostly Darcy, but you don't stop her. By the way, she phoned asking me to babysit. I'm sure you had her say I can't invite Ryan to her house."

Rebecca's casual shrug was the same as an admission. "You turned her down?"

"No, but I have a question. How will her boys or

Jordan learn to be good husbands and fathers if all they hear is you and Darcy griping about the men you married?"

"I beg your pardon? When have I ever *griped* about your father?"

"If he's not a sleaze, why can't we see him? I'll bet he left because you nagged. Or maybe because you cheated on him."

"I don't owe you any explanation, young lady. And as for me being unfaithful…that's not even close. Anyway, this isn't about me, Lisa. It's about you. I work two jobs so you can have a stable life. You need to do your part by not letting your grades slip."

"Everything always comes back to you and your jobs."

"Yes, it does. I make no secret of the fact that my lack of education was a drawback. That's why I nag you. A woman, especially, needs college so she can support a family should her marriage fail. You've seen how many marriages fall apart."

"But all my friends at school have boyfriends, and they're still planning to go to college. Ryan Lane is the nicest boy I've ever met. You can't stop me from seeing him. If I can't bring him home, Mother, I'll meet him someplace else." Grabbing her books, Lisa stalked from the room.

Rebecca sagged. So much for thinking she could reason with her daughter. Come hell or high water, she needed to contact Ryan Lane's father.

CHAPTER TWO

DURING A BREAK between morning clients at the salon the following week, Rebecca called Lisa's school counselor. Mrs. Feldman agreed with Rebecca that Lisa's infatuation with Ryan Lane was probably the main reason behind Lisa's slipping grades. As they chatted, Rebecca found out a bit more about the Lane family. Grant Lane had recently retired from the air force as a colonel and moved to San Antonio with his two children, Ryan and a young daughter, Brandy.

After the conversation with the counselor, Rebecca got the Lanes' number from directory assistance. Determined to solve this issue parent-to-parent, Rebecca dialed before she could get cold feet.

GRANT LANE, who'd just transferred a load of his daughter's clothes from the washer to the dryer, walked into his kitchen to pour his first cup of morning coffee. The phone rang. He grabbed it, worried that something had happened to Ryan or Brandy.

"Hello."

"Mr. Lane, my name is Rebecca Geroux. I don't know if you're aware, but your son, Ryan, and my daughter, Lisa, seem to be dating. Until recently, my daughter was a straight-A student. Now her grades are slipping, and I believe it's because she's infatuated with your son."

"I'm sorry, who is this?"

"I'm Lisa Geroux's mother, Rebecca. I'm calling from work, so unfortunately I can't talk long. The thing is, Mr. Lane, Lisa needs to keep her grades up in order to qualify for college scholarships. Frankly, Ryan is a huge distraction. I'm appealing to you, hoping you'll influence him."

Grant took a slug of the hot coffee to jump-start his brain and let him piece together the choppy facts the woman threw at him. It was news to him that Ryan had a girlfriend. They weren't exactly on the greatest terms. Anyhow, Ryan was almost eighteen. Grant would worry if he *didn't* have girlfriends. "Well, Mrs. Geroux, I'm happy to hear Ryan has made friends, being new in San Antonio and all."

"This is getting out of hand. Lisa's never cared for sports, and now she's throwing away valuable study time watching your son play baseball. It's also come to my attention that after the game, when Lisa's supposed to be babysitting for one of my co-workers, Ryan takes her—well, all of them—to a fast-food restaurant where they waste several hours she could use for studying. Are you saying this isn't affecting Ryan's schoolwork?"

"Not that I've seen. Ryan's always been a good student." Grant wasn't about to tell this woman, a perfect stranger, that his son didn't confide in him and he had no idea what Ryan's grades were like. Their rapport had never been great, and it'd gotten worse since Grant's retirement—when he'd really become a full-time dad.

But maybe he could find out more from Mrs. Geroux. He cleared his throat. "I can see you're better informed about all of this than I am. Tell you what, I'd be willing to meet with you and your husband to explore this further. Of course, it'll have to be when Ryan's not around. Or his sister. I have a younger daughter, and it's just me. I mean, I'm a single parent."

"So am I. Meeting you could be difficult, which is why I phoned. I work two jobs, Mr. Lane, so I don't have much free time."

"Please…call me Grant. I really do think we need to discuss this in more depth. I'm not convinced I want to interfere in my son's school friendships."

"Shoot, my next client just arrived. I need to hang up and go back to work, uh…Grant. I have to say I'm disappointed. I assumed you'd work with me once I explained the situation."

Grant fiddled with his coffee cup. Mrs. Geroux's displeasure was telegraphed clearly, and he felt bad for her. "Is it possible for you to get away from work for an hour or so tomorrow? I'll give you my address. If you can drop by here, you can follow me to our neighborhood café. We can talk over coffee or breakfast if you'd like to meet before work."

"Tomorrow might be okay. What time? I'll need to move or cancel clients, but I'm serious about getting Lisa back on track."

"How does nine-fifteen sound?"

"I'll make it work. It's that important, Mr. Lane."

"Grant," he reminded her. Then gave her his address and precise directions. After he hung up, Grant wondered if he'd regret offering to meet Rebecca Geroux. What if she turned out to be a lunatic? But it was the only way he could buy time to figure out a response. How would it have sounded if he'd admitted he didn't even know Ryan was playing baseball, let alone that he had a girlfriend?

Obviously his relationship with his son needed attention, and it was also plain that the Geroux woman thought he could influence Ryan. For that to happen, he and his son would have to have a civil face-to-face talk. Grant would welcome one, but things had happened over Ryan's lifetime to erect barriers between them. He wasn't sure he knew how to break them down.

Grant wondered what Rebecca Geroux would think of a father who was on such a rocky footing with his eldest child. He reflected on the cause for his problems with Ryan. He could probably go all the way back to before Teresa died, when his obsession with flying and his career took precedence over his marriage. He'd failed to see how his wife's troubled history affected their firstborn. For so long it had seemed easier to stay away and avoid the un-happiness—his and Teresa's. All that time Teresa had raised Ryan alone, and he'd let her, because it was easier to be off building his career.

He supposed he was still looking for the easy way out.

WHEN REBECCA got home after work, she toyed with the idea of calling Mr. Lane back and canceling. After all, they should be able to come to an agreement over the phone. She formulated what she'd say to him as she stopped to collect the mail. Absently, she tore open and inspected the bank statement from the joint college savings account she held with Lisa. Rebecca noted her deposits listed for each week of the month. Lisa, though, hadn't contributed a thing. Not one cent in nearly five weeks.

The paper fluttered in Rebecca's hand as she tried to absorb the information. She sat for a moment before stuffing the statement back in its envelope. Then she took a deep breath in an effort to calm her temper. Why no deposits, when Lisa had started babysitting for Darcy and was earning more than in previous months?

Rebecca called the kids and started fixing supper. Once they were all seated at the table, she let them fill their plates before she pulled the statement out of her pocket. Rebecca laid it in front of Lisa, who blanched.

"Mom, I have a year and a half before I need to pay college tuition."

"True, but each year the costs go up. What disturbs me, Lisa, is that we had a deal. Why didn't you follow through?"

"I had school expenses," Lisa mumbled. "Stuff my friends can get without a hassle. I haven't asked you for money. Why do I have to explain what I'm buying?"

"*What* things do you need, Lisa? This is the first I've heard of any of this. I don't want you kids to go without. I want you to fit in."

Lisa got up, leaving her supper untouched on the table. "I'm so sick of money being such an issue. Our garbage disposal is still broken, Mother. Ryan would've fixed it at no charge." Without waiting for a response, she stormed off toward her bedroom.

Ryan again. Rebecca swirled her peas and carrots through her steamed rice. She'd lost her appetite, too.

Jordan ate everything on his plate, but kept his head down until he reached for seconds and then noticed his mom's listlessness. "Lisa bought an athletic booster card for baseball season so she could get a discount on the game tickets. And the girls I see her hang with have loads more cash to throw around."

"Who are these girls? Do I know them or are they new friends she's met with Ryan?"

Jordan shrugged. He finished his meal, then he,

too, disappeared. By the time Rebecca tidied up and left for her job at the Tumbleweed, both kids were in their rooms, and she was once again convinced that she had to meet Grant Lane.

THE NEXT MORNING Rebecca gave herself two hours to meet Ryan's father and enlist his help in breaking up their kids. She hadn't handled yesterday's conversation very well. He'd sounded as if he favored Ryan and Lisa being a couple. It was up to her to convince him otherwise.

Rebecca tried to anticipate how their discussion might go if he continued to oppose her. Well, it wouldn't be a surprise. Grant Lane probably thought his son was a great catch.

And rightly so, she admitted grudgingly. Rebecca couldn't blame Lisa for thinking that Ryan was hot. His eyes were a clear, arresting blue, framed by lashes most girls would kill for. Add his cool car to all that, and any girl would be impressed.

Again, Rebecca turned her thoughts to the father. What kind of man bought his teenage son a convertible? Grant must have bought it, because Ryan clearly didn't work. It would help if he did.

Some men had skewed values. Jack, for example. The only reason Rebecca was willing to meet with a strange man was to ensure that Lisa was better equipped to deal with the Jack Geroux types than she'd been. That was why she'd canceled two clients who hadn't been able to come in later. Rebecca could see money flying out the window, and she'd have to juggle her bills again. Did single dads have as much difficulty making ends meet?

For the first time Rebecca wondered what had happened to Ryan's mother. Most likely she'd died, since the kids lived with their dad. Rebecca caught herself momentarily feeling sorry for the children. For Grant Lane, too. Single parenting was hard, regardless of the circumstances.

Lost in her thoughts, Rebecca almost missed the entry to the Lanes' housing development. Reading off street names, she found the one she was looking for, and made a right turn onto a tree-lined avenue. The homes were spacious, and their landscaping immaculate. Rebecca's house would fit twice into any one of these Spanish-style mansions. But somehow, after seeing Ryan Lane's convertible, the affluent neighborhood didn't surprise her. No doubt the boy had been born into money, and had a future loaded with potential.

She hoped Lisa wasn't dazzled by all the material things beyond her reach. Frowning, Rebecca braked in front of a driveway that led up to a sprawling house. Multiple arches, red-tile roof, a pristine lawn. The number matched the address Grant Lane had given her.

She wished she'd suggested they just meet at the café he'd mentioned. Her hands felt damp and slippery on the steering wheel. Wouldn't it be awkward going up to knock on a strange man's door—especially here, where she was so out of her element? Grant had a nice, melodic voice, she reminded herself. Rebecca hoped he had a personality to match it.

Even as she debated turning around, the decision was taken out of her hands.

The front door opened and every thought sailed right out of her head. The elder Lane came halfway down his brick walkway to pick up his paper. To say he was good-looking was too tame.

Rebecca's heart thudded. As she tried to settle it, he came up to her car and gestured for her to roll down her window.

"Are you Rebecca Geroux, or just lost in the neighborhood?"

His eyes crinkled at the corners when he smiled, and Rebecca managed to say, "I'm Rebecca."

"Good. Let me throw my paper in the house. My car's in the garage. I'll back out and you can follow me."

Rebecca had noticed the dark blue SUV in the driveway when she drove up. Now she wondered if that was also his, or if Grant Lane was seeing someone. Although if he was, it didn't matter to her.

Watching him jog back to the house, Rebecca admitted she'd been expecting someone older. He couldn't have more than a few years on her. Surely a man his age must still work.

She waited, and finally the garage door lifted.

Rebecca wrenched on the ignition, giving silent thanks when the Nissan purred to life. She'd just released the parking brake when a red sports car shot out past the SUV. Grant punched a remote control hanging on his sun visor and the door lowered.

Rebecca admired the Porsche Boxter convertible as it sped off down the road. She gave herself a shake. Here she sat drooling like an idiot, and he'd turned the corner at the end of the block. She barely managed to get under way and keep him in sight. He navigated the suburban streets with confidence.

Rebecca thought she'd lost him after he pulled into an area of strip malls. She caught him at a light and saw that he was signaling a turn into a parking space in front of a brightly lit café she would otherwise have missed.

She pulled in farther down the street, but couldn't help noticing that Grant was already out of his car. Reaching back in, he hung his sunglasses over the visor.

Boy, he was trusting, leaving his top down and his expensive shades in plain sight. She'd installed motion detectors around her house, and attached a Club to her steering wheel every night to discourage car theft. But that was the difference between her neighborhood and Grant Lane's.

He waited for her beside the café door. As she walked toward Grant, Rebecca cataloged more things about him. His hair was shorter than his son's and not as dark—more of a honey shade, thick and sun-streaked. But it wasn't as short as the military types she saw around town. And there were a lot of those, as San Antonio was home to many military families. The slightly mussed style suited him. He wore khaki pants and a navy-blue T-shirt that showed off toned muscles. He looked…darn good. Suntanned. Carefree.

Rebecca glanced at her reflection in the café window to see if she appeared as harried as she felt. Satisfied that she looked okay, she reminded herself that she couldn't stay long. Her first client was booked for eleven-thirty.

Smiling again, Grant opened the restaurant door wider, allowing Rebecca to pass. It was a nice touch and she gave him points for being a gentleman.

"Thank you," she murmured.

"I usually sit in a booth by the window, but why don't we get a table at the back where we can talk more freely?" He gestured for her to go first. Rebecca felt conspicuous in her work clothes and comfy shoes, but she refused to slouch.

The waitress arrived seconds after they sat down. "I thought you'd skipped breakfast today," she said to Grant. "Do you want the usual? And what about the lady?"

"Just coffee for me. Black, one sugar," Rebecca said.

"Make it the same for me." Grant turned over both cups that already sat on the table.

Pasting on a smile, Rebecca gripped the handle of her cup. "I'll pay for my coffee," she said.

He frowned. "Not necessary. I invited you." He followed that with another smile of his own that sent heat all the way to Rebecca's toes. For a moment, her carefully prepared speech lodged in her throat.

"I'll get right to the point, if I may," she said, refocusing her attention. "Your son seems to be a good kid, but he's all wrong for my daughter. Perhaps I wasn't clear, but she's a junior and this year is very important. If she has any shot at scholarships, her grades must remain exemplary. I've had no luck convincing her to stop seeing Ryan. I thought that, as another single parent, you might understand and help by persuading Ryan to move on. Lisa has to focus on school. That's all there is to it."

"At their age, shouldn't they have a say in how they spend their free time and who they spend it with? I mean, she sounds like a wonderful girl. One a father would be happy to have his son date."

"You don't get it at all." Rebecca twirled her cup around and around. "She's spent money she can't afford on a pass for Ryan's ball games. Money that should be going into her college fund."

"Why isn't she doing what you ask?"

Rebecca's eyes flashed. "I suppose because she's flattered by his attention. She's not used to it. The new boy. An athlete. All of that gives her social standing, according to my son."

"How old is he? Doesn't he have any influence with his sister?"

"Apparently not." Rebecca held her cup so tightly her knuckles turned white. "I honestly thought I'd taught Lisa the importance of a good education." Sipping her coffee, Rebecca shook her head sadly.

"Choosing to watch a high school ball game isn't the end of the world. So she gets a little off-track. Don't all kids do that at least once? Or have you planned for every contingency and lived a perfect, orderly life?"

"Hardly. Which is why I want more for my children. But this isn't about me. It's about making sure our teens stay on the right path."

Grant shrugged.

"Is that your answer? Maybe this doesn't matter to you, but it matters to me." Rebecca slid out of the booth, dug in her purse and slapped two one-dollar bills down on the table. "Thanks for nothing." She stormed out of the café, got in her car and pulled into traffic, all the while muttering under her breath about what a jerk Grant Lane was.

GRANT WATCHED Rebecca leave in a huff. He sat glaring after her. She had some nerve trying to manipulate him into a confrontation with Ryan when her own daughter wouldn't listen to a word she'd said. Although maybe she'd inadvertently handed him a way to bond with his son. If Ryan liked the girl, and she liked him, why shouldn't they date? It was what normal teens did.

He paid for his coffee, and followed in Rebecca's wake. She'd already gone through the light at the corner by the time he climbed into his car.

The flash of her ocean-colored eyes haunted Grant as he eased the Boxter into traffic. The hell of it was she'd managed to garner his sympathy, too. He thought about Brandy. If he were in Rebecca's position and it was his daughter getting into a romance with her son, Grant had to admit he might feel differently. He knew well enough that sometimes a young man was ruled by baser instincts. Rebecca probably knew, too.

But didn't she trust her daughter?

Adjusting his sunglasses, Grant stopped to wonder why Mrs. Geroux didn't just ground her daughter, the almost-genius, if she was really that concerned.

It irritated Grant all over again as he replayed their conversation and realized Rebecca had made it seem as if Ryan was totally to blame for leading the brilliant Lisa astray. What if Rebecca had a skewed vision of her daughter?

By all reports his son was a good student, although if truth be told, Grant couldn't claim much credit for it. Still, Lisa wasn't the only one who'd be going to college.

This full-time-dad role also meant Grant ought to concern himself with what kind of friends Ryan hung out with. Who knew better than he how easily a young man could screw up his life?

Did Lisa Geroux look like her mother? Rebecca

was attractive. Especially when she was passionately standing up for her daughter. Grant hadn't exactly processed all of Rebecca's complaints, because he'd been distracted by her pretty eyes and lush lips. She made quite the picture with her shoulder-length red hair curled in wild disarray around her face. Grant found he'd been most drawn to Rebecca's eyes. They held fire and life, yet he saw a hint of tragedy in their luminous depths.

For the first time in a long while, a woman—a slightly brusque one who didn't care for him at that—had provoked a yearning Grant had thought was dormant, if not dead. He'd purposely avoided serious relationships since his ordeal with Teresa.

Why had he let Rebecca leave so abruptly? His day now stretched before him like all the lonely days he'd experienced since he'd moved his family to San Antonio. He needed a hobby. Something more than writing a new technical strategy manual as an old friend now in the Pentagon had asked him to do. He'd thought retirement would let him connect with his kids, but they seemed remarkably self-sufficient.

What would Rebecca have said if he'd asked her to go out with him some night? Nothing to do with their kids.

He could guess. She'd already blown up at him. Grant grinned at the thought of what it'd be like to intentionally stoke her fire.

She'd also given up on him too fast. After his

years in the military, Grant took his time to make an informed decision. If she wanted his help, she should've given him more information. He needed to talk to her again.

But he supposed he'd have to get her phone number from Ryan.

Grant swung his car into his driveway and impatiently punched the garage door opener that hung on his visor. The problem with having to question his son, as Grant knew only too well, was that Ryan barely spoke to him.

Rebecca of the captivating eyes and the protective love for her daughter clearly expected him to be able to influence his son's choices.

What were the chances of that?

For too many years he'd left raising Ryan to Teresa. With all the ups and downs in their marriage, it had seemed easier. The result hadn't turned out well for anyone.

Considering his lack of rapport with Ryan, Grant knew he couldn't open a conversation by repeating Rebecca's accusations. Especially when he'd been clueless when it came to Ryan's friends. Or girlfriends, for that matter.

He wasn't ready to admit the girl was a problem, but wasn't keeping tabs on stuff like that an important part of parenting? He hadn't been good at it in the past, but had vowed to be better after their move. It seemed he had a lot of catching up to do.

Thank God Brandy still thought he was an okay dad. But with Ryan he'd have to tread carefully. Very, very carefully.

But he didn't intend to wade into those waters alone. Rebecca Geroux's daughter made up the other half of the so-called relationship. Becca— Grant thought that name fit the firebrand better than starchy *Rebecca*—yes, Becca could damn well get her feet wet right alongside him.

If she hadn't mentioned it on the phone yesterday, Grant wouldn't have known his son was playing ball until he overheard Ryan let something slip this morning to his sister.

It was usually Ryan's job to pick up his sister from school. Lately, though, he'd gotten into the habit of leaving notes on the fridge asking Grant to collect her several days a week. Grant hadn't asked why. All the reports he'd ever had on Ryan in Germany said he was a good, studious kid. Grant had assumed, apparently incorrectly, that changing schools during Ryan's senior year required extra work in the library. Grant hadn't pressed for answers because he was glad of the additional time to bond with the daughter who'd been raised too long by nannies. Yet another mistake.

Just today, Ryan had told Brandy where he'd be after school. At a home baseball game. It hurt to learn that Ryan had deliberately kept this a secret.

What better place to begin catching up on his son's life? Ryan probably wouldn't be thrilled to see him, but having the element of surprise on his side was an advantage.

Grant focused on his ideas for the manual, killing time until he needed to get Brandy from school.

"Hi, kiddo," he said, his heart lighter when she hugged him after tossing her pink backpack in the backseat. Grant was driving the SUV, preferring its side airbags whenever he had his kids with him. The Porsche was an indulgence. A guy thing, although Ryan referred to it as an upside-down bathtub. A pretty pricy bathtub even with the deep discount he'd got by purchasing it at the factory in Germany.

Brandy fastened her seat belt, and turned her big blue eyes on Grant. "Daddy, can I get a clarinet? The band teacher came to our homeroom today. He tested everybody in my grade on flute, clarinet and two horns. One with a slidy thing, the other with three buttons on top. Mr. Gregg—that's the teacher's name—said to tell you I have the perfect embouchure to play clarinet."

She said it so proudly Grant couldn't help smiling, even though he had no earthly idea what she meant. "That's great, Brandy. Did Mr. Gregg suggest renting a clarinet to see if it's something you really want to do?"

"Uh-huh. But most kids are going to have their parents buy new ones. Who wants to use someone else's mouthpiece? Gross!"

"I see your point. I'll look into it next week and see what they have at a music store. Right now, how would you like to go to the high school to watch your brother play baseball?"

Brandy's eyes grew wide. "Does Ryan know you're going to watch him pitch?"

"So he's a pitcher. I'll be…" Grant let the expletive fizzle on his tongue. "You knew he was playing ball?"

"He played in Germany, too. He's good, Daddy."

"Then there's no reason for us not to go watch him, is there?"

She brushed blond curls off her face. "I don't want him to think I ratted on him."

"Honestly, Brandy." Grant blew out a frustrated breath. "Parents are entitled to know what activities their kids are into."

Her little pixie face fell, and Grant immediately softened his tone. "Maybe he won't spot us. But if he does, I'll make sure he knows we're there because he mentioned it this morning."

"I guess it'll be okay, then."

Grant located the ball diamond and parked a distance from the gate. As he and Brandy walked along the fence, Grant peered through the mesh, trying to get the lay of the land, so to speak. It appeared the home team was at bat. There were already a lot of people in the stands, making it easier to pay and slip in unnoticed.

"There's Ryan, Daddy! He's coming up to bat." Brandy spoke so loudly several people turned to look at them. Grant's gaze lit on an attractive strawberry-blonde. Her hair was as curly as Brandy's, but shorter. Finding seats in the second row from the top, Grant eyed the girl, who appeared to have her hands full with two younger children. Twins, would be his guess. Tough, active little boys. Their antics made Grant smile. But he also felt sorry for the girl, who must be their sister or babysitter. When two older boys raced up and flung their arms around her neck, he wondered how on earth she managed to handle all four.

Grant was intrigued by the way all four boys and the blond girl had their attention on Ryan, who was indeed at bat. Ryan slugged a home run on the second pitch. The quintet in the front row clapped madly and yelled Ryan's name. Even more intriguing was what happened two seconds after Ryan jogged triumphantly across home plate. The twins charged right over to him. Grant watched his son scoop both boys up, then, grinning like a hyena, join the blond girl on the sidelines.

Grant muttered under his breath. The girl had to be Lisa Geroux. Her flashing aquamarine eyes reminded Grant of her mother. And there was no mistaking the chemistry she and Ryan shared. The joy vanished from Ryan's face the instant the girl turned and pointed to him and Brandy.

Busted, Grant thought guiltily. She must have heard Brandy's loud comment when they arrived. His stomach bottomed out the way it did when he pulled too many Gs in flight. Ryan *was* involved with a girl. And her mother was dead set against the relationship. What a mess. He could've retired any number of places, but he'd picked San Antonio. It'd been his first duty station and held some happy memories. He'd hoped his kids would like it here, and that maybe he and Ryan could heal old wounds.

Now it appeared they could be facing more problems than ever. It was evident they needed to talk about a lot of things. Not here in front of a crowd, but soon.

Standing, Grant took Brandy's hand. Ignoring her protests, he led her to the side of the bleachers farthest away from where Ryan stood glaring at them. Grant jumped down and held up his arms for Brandy.

"Why are we leaving? We never got to watch Ryan pitch."

"Turns out this wasn't a good idea, Brandy. How about we go get ice cream instead?"

"Rocky road?"

"Sure." It would no doubt ruin her appetite for dinner. Here he went again, being far too easygoing. But he couldn't have both his kids hating him. Maybe he should get a few pointers on tough parenting from Rebecca Geroux.

CHAPTER THREE

RYAN LANE stormed into his house around five o'clock, radiating belligerence. Grant had anticipated the outburst, which was why he'd made arrangements for Brandy to play at the home of a new school friend.

Grant looked up from the couch and marked his place in the Dale Brown book he was reading.

"What the hell were you doing this afternoon?" Ryan threw his duffel bag on the couch, barely missing his dad.

"Watch your language, and I suggest you rethink using that tone with me, Ryan."

The angry teen showed no inclination to back down. Hands splayed on his hips, Ryan ignored his father's suggestion. "You haven't given a damn about anything I've done for seventeen years. I don't want or need you poking your nose in my business now."

"You're wrong about my not caring." Setting his book on the lamp stand, Grant stood. He still had three inches and a few pounds on his gangly, six-foot son. He recognized the show of testosterone, but Grant was determined to remain cool and in control.

"Right!" Ryan raised his voice. "You paid housekeepers and nannies, and that means you cared?"

Grant scraped a finger over the stubble on his chin. "I made sure I hired the most qualified caregivers I could find. My job made it impossible to be a full-time dad. You know, son, I don't think that's what's bugging you now. Why don't you tell me what you're really upset about?"

"I want you to get off my back."

"Coming to see you play ball is being on your back? Did you win, by the way?"

"No! My pitching went to hell after Lisa pointed you out in the stands."

"About her..." Grant hesitated, choosing his words carefully. "She and her brothers were certainly excited about your home run."

"They aren't her brothers. Lisa babysits them." Ryan acted as if his father was short on brain cells. "Their mother works with Lisa's," he snapped. "Lisa's only sixteen, but she's in all my honors classes. Her brother's a freshman. Not that I have to explain anything to you about my friends or their families."

Grant slid his fists deep in his front pockets. Belatedly he remembered Rebecca mentioning that her daughter babysat. "Ryan, I realize our family isn't the most conventional. At Ramstein, because it was a closed community, I knew the parents of all your friends. Living off base is an adjustment. I'd hoped it would give us the chance to…get more in touch with each other, for lack of a better term. That's why I bought a house with a patio and a pool. I want us to do things together."

"Like, you suddenly think we'll have barbecues and be best buds?"

"For starters, you could invite your friends over some weekend…with their parents," he added as an afterthought. "I assume your friend Lisa has parents."

Ryan scowled. "Lisa works most weekends. And Mrs. Geroux isn't overly friendly. It's a bad idea, all right?" He snatched up his duffel. "Besides, it's just Lisa, her mom and her brother, Jordan. So drop it, okay?"

Grant heard Ryan clomp down the tiled hall to his room. His door slammed, and instantly the house pulsed with the sounds of the Red Hot Chili Peppers. Grant shut his eyes, took a deep breath and reminded himself that Ryan was still just a kid. A kid who'd had too much autonomy for too long. That was Grant's fault.

In sudden need of air, he fled to the patio. He'd hired a pool service, but brushing off the day's accumulation of dust from the pool's pebbly sides helped clear his mind. He didn't think he could be of any use to Rebecca Geroux. Not without widening the rift between him and Ryan. Grant had been aware of their rift even before Teresa died. His dilemma had always been that he didn't know what to say—didn't know how to explain his and Teresa's marital problems to a boy who worshipped his mother. And was it too late to explain it all now?

Crap! Let Rebecca Geroux solve her problems by herself. Lord knew he had enough of his own. Problems that dated back to when he wasn't much older than his son.

Teresa had come into his life at a bad time. They shouldn't have stayed married, but she didn't want a divorce. And her mental and physical health had been fragile, or so Grant assumed. Too late he discovered a lot had been manipulation.

Whether she meant to or not, Teresa had let her histrionics drive a wedge between father and son. And after her untimely death, Grant's guilt kept him even farther from Ryan. He'd floundered, and that wasn't the military way. So, he'd put the problem out of his mind.

Grant hung the pool brush on its pegs and headed back to the house. He should probably find Rebecca and explain why he couldn't help her break the kids up. He also wasn't happy with the way he'd let her leave the café.

After more internal debate, he decided to phone her. Since asking Ryan for the number wasn't an option now, he turned to the phone book. Only no Rebecca or R. Geroux was listed in the San Antonio telephone directory. Thank heaven for the Internet. It was a little scary to see how easily he turned up her supposedly unlisted number.

Grant shut his bedroom door to make the call in private—not that Ryan would hear anything over the blaring music. On his first attempt, Grant misdialed. On the second try, a boy answered. Grant remembered Ryan's saying Lisa had a brother. "May I speak with Rebecca?" he asked.

"She's at work. Who's calling, please?"

"A friend. I suppose I could drop by and see her there."

"Yeah, sure. Anyone can eat at the Tumbleweed. But she's always busy."

Grant heard someone in the background ask who was on the phone. The boy obviously covered the mouthpiece before saying, "Some dude wants Mom. Okay, okay, Lisa. Uh…I've gotta go," the kid said. And he hung up.

The Tumbleweed wasn't hard to find in the directory. The place was open until ten, which gave Grant plenty of time to get the kids some takeout once Brandy got home. He just had to come up with a good excuse for leaving after dinner.

Greeting her at the door when her friend's mother dropped her off, he took in his daughter's smiling face. "Did you have fun with Kiley?"

"Uh-huh. She has a puppy. He's *so* cute. Can I get one?"

"We'll see. Puppies need a lot of care and attention."

"I know. Kiley's mama said puppies are like babies. The vet gave Kiley a book that's got everything a pet owner needs to know. She said I can borrow it. I'll bet Ryan would help me."

"Help you what?" Brandy's brother suddenly appeared in the kitchen doorway.

"My friend Kiley has a new shih tzu. I'm trying to talk Daddy into getting me a puppy from the same breeder."

"I'd rather have a real dog. Like a shepherd," Ryan said. "I came out to see when dinner is. I'm starved. What are we eating tonight?"

Grant reached for a folder of take-out menus. "I thought pizza. You two decide what kind." He hesitated. He ought to eat with the kids. But then what excuse could he give Rebecca for going to the Tumbleweed? "I'll place the order and give you the money to pay the delivery boy. I have an errand to run. I'll grab something while I'm out."

"What kind of errand?" Ryan asked, sounding suspicious. "You haven't gone out at night by yourself since we moved here."

Ignoring Ryan, Grant passed the pizza menu to his daughter.

Brandy wrinkled her nose. "Why can't we have real food, Daddy? Kiley's mom was baking chicken and it smelled so yummy."

"That's what moms do, kid," Ryan said, plucking the menu from her hand. "Dads are pretty much worthless in the kitchen."

"I beg your pardon. Some of the world's greatest chefs are men," Grant protested.

"*You,* then," Ryan stressed. "Why don't you hire a cook like you did in Germany?"

Brandy climbed onto one of the breakfast-bar stools. "I don't want a cook. I want a mom."

"Brandy, don't be a dork. Moms aren't as easy to get as puppies."

"I am not a dork, Ryan," Brandy said huffily. "Our room mom, Mrs. Sanchez, is supernice, Daddy. I'll bet you'd like her. Manny Sanchez says it's awful not having a dad to help at home."

Ryan smacked his sister lightly on the head with the menu. "You are so lame. For parents to hook up they have to meet, hold hands and kiss. Can you picture Dad kissing your room mom—or anyone else?"

"All right, you two," Grant said loudly. "Enough with trying to arrange my love life. What kind of pizza will it be tonight?"

"Hamburger and tomato," Ryan said. "And I wasn't arranging anything. I was explaining to Brandy how low the chances are that any woman would want to date you."

Grant glared at his son as he dialed the pizza parlor's number. "I'd like to place an order. One large tomato-hamburger pizza for delivery." When he hung up, he realized Ryan's declaration had shaken him. Grant had never considered himself vain. However, as he set out money for the pizza it was all he could do not to recheck his appearance in the mirror. How would Rebecca Geroux see him?

But he refused to admit any interest in the woman beyond explaining that he really couldn't help her.

"I'll be back before Brandy's bedtime," he muttered, his hand on the doorknob.

"Will you look at puppies while you're out?" Brandy pleaded. "Oh, and remember you said you'd look at clarinets."

"Not tonight, honey. We'll make time for that soon, though."

Ryan glanced up from returning the menu to the take-out folder. "I have plans for the last weekend next month. Saturday afternoon and evening," he said. "I thought I'd tell you in advance since you didn't bother to ask if I was busy tonight. You just expect me to watch Brandy anytime it suits you."

"I'm sorry, Ryan. If you have plans, I can do this another night." Grant, who was partway out the door, turned back.

Ryan was obviously spoiling for a fight, and his flustered backtracking was almost comical. "I'm staying in tonight," he mumbled. "But from here on, you'd better check with me first, all right?"

"That's fair, Ryan. I want us all to get along."

"Well, okay then," the boy said, sounding surprised.

AFTER REVERSING his car out to the street, Grant massaged the tension from his neck. He shouldn't have waited so long to start being a father to his kids. Work had always been his excuse. Now he had to feel his way through the minefield that Ryan, especially, delighted in laying down.

At the first turn, Grant punched the address for the Tumbleweed Steakhouse into his GPS, and he thought about seeing Rebecca again. How long had she been on her own? he wondered. Long enough to be back to dating? For all he knew she might already be seeing someone.

He found the restaurant easily enough, but hesitated about going inside. He wasn't at all confident as to how he'd be received.

The minute he crossed the threshold, he spotted her. She didn't see him, so he helped himself to a table near the door and noted what had attracted him earlier. The fiery hair had all but crackled in the sunlight that streamed in the café window that morning. Now, under the overhead lights, it was more muted, but still shone.

As she joked with customers two tables away, Grant liked how her eyes stayed bright with interest in what the older couple was saying. Making people feel important was a gift. Grant quickly opened a menu he found on his table to distract himself from an unexpected rush of heat.

He heard her footsteps approach, then halt as she recognized her next customer.

"I haven't come to cause trouble," he assured her, meeting her startled gaze.

"Why come at all?" Her low voice hit him hard. "You made your position plain enough earlier."

"We need to talk further."

"Not here," she said uneasily. "I'm working, for pity's sake."

"Where then?"

She tucked her order pad in the pocket of a cow-print apron. "There's an outdoor coffee shop on the next block." She jerked her head. "I'm due a fifteen-minute break soon, but you go on ahead. I'll ask another waitress to cover my tables."

"Is this your way of getting rid of me?"

"I wouldn't do that," she insisted. "I'll be along shortly. You can order me an iced coffee."

Grant had been looking forward to one of those steaks that made his mouth water. And the talk he'd had in mind would probably take more than fifteen minutes. But he supposed even this much was a start.

Unfolding from his chair, he ambled out. From the corner of his eye, he saw Rebecca pull aside a blond waitress in a matching apron. Ouch, he could almost feel the glare that one sent him with her flinty gray eyes.

As he shut the door behind him, he remembered Ryan's remark about the four little boys at the game belonging to someone Rebecca worked with. The boys were blond, too, so it fit. Grant peeked in through the window, wondering how much Rebecca would tell her friend about him. Most of his concern was about how quickly Ryan might hear of this meeting. He'd see this as his dad going behind his back.

Nothing to be done about that now.

Grant found the coffee shop easily enough. He bought them each a coffee and claimed a table away from the foot traffic on the River Walk. He'd barely set napkins under the cups when Rebecca slid gracefully into the chair across from him at the small, wrought-iron table. A lantern hanging from the brick building rained golden light down on her, accenting distinctive cheekbones.

Suddenly a light, flower-scented perfume had him imagining secret meetings in more intimate settings.

"So, talk already," she said, peeling the lid off her coffee cup. "I don't have long. I hope you're here to say you've had second thoughts, and that you were able to convince your son to break up with my daughter."

He shook his head, as much to focus his mind as to deny having any success.

She took a sip of coffee, and frowned. "Then what's this all about?"

Grant set his cup down. "Why are you so set on meddling in their lives?" he asked, leaning toward her. "Do you hate all men, or just those interested in your daughter?"

"How dare you judge me!" Rebecca stiffened noticeably.

"I asked Ryan if he'd like to invite some of his friends and their parents to our house for a barbecue. I hoped it would open up a dialogue and maybe he'd mention Lisa. Ryan said you weren't overly friendly."

"I *was* rude." She blew out a sigh. "I'd just learned that Lisa's grades were slipping. I believe it's because she's smitten with your son. I want so much more for her. For her and my son, Jordan."

"And 'more' doesn't include falling in love and getting married?"

Rebecca's eyes flashed angrily, and Grant held up a hand. "Whoa! Don't get me wrong. I have no idea how tight Ryan and Lisa are. We agree on one thing, though. I don't want my son getting married at his age, either. So far as I know, he's college-bound, too."

"So far as you know? He should've applied and been accepted somewhere by now."

Grant fought to contain his irritation. "So maybe fathers and sons don't share confidences like moms and daughters do."

She studied him over the rim of her cup. "Lisa and I used to be close. She's changed. It's not just the grades and the boyfriend. Recently she lashed out at me, saying her father wouldn't be as mean as I am. That hurt a lot."

Silence stretched between them. "Then you're divorced?"

"Yes. Since Lisa was two. Jordan's never even seen his father."

"Shouldn't he be involved? Instead of coming to me for help, maybe you should be going to him."

"That's not an option. I know it sounds cold to you, and I don't expect you to understand. I did hear somewhere that your wife died, which makes our situations completely different."

Grant took a swig of his coffee. "How do you figure that?"

"The saga of my marriage would take way more time than we have." Rebecca glanced at her watch. "I need to get back to work."

"And we still don't have a solution to your problem. I think our kids have a big date at the end of next month."

"A big date? Doing what?"

"I'm not sure. I'll see if I can find out. Maybe we should meet again after I do. Could be just a harmless outing." Grant twirled his cup in aimless circles. "Rebecca, I'll tell you something I was reluctant to bring up earlier. I have a...bumpy relationship with my son. I wondered if you might have some tips about how I could get closer to him. If I can do that, I'd have more influence." He held up a hand. "I know that look. Just spit it out. You think I'm a bad father."

"I wasn't thinking that at all. I saw where you live. Your kids have a good life. Nice house. Nice cars. You're retired at what...fortyish?"

"Forty-two. Feels like more," he joked.

"Well, you look like life's treated you fine," Rebecca drawled. "Oh, I'm sorry. I completely forgot about your wife's death. Sometimes I speak before I think."

His expression darkened a moment. "Listen, I'll

keep it short, but you seem to have gotten the wrong impression. It sounds like we've both had our troubles."

Grant's hands tightened around his cup, and he cleared his throat. "I grew up in Virginia. All I ever wanted to do was fly airplanes. I couldn't get into the Air Force Academy because my family didn't have the political connections. I went to college and applied to officers' candidate school instead. While I was waiting to hear, I fell in with a party crowd. My folks gave me grief, but on weekends I tended to bunk at the frat house even though I'd already graduated. One night they threw a really wild party with plenty of booze. All the sorority girls came, and one latched on to me. Teresa. We got smashed, and she smuggled me into her dorm room for the night. That pretty much says it all, but we avoided each other after that. A few weeks later, on the day I heard I'd been accepted into an air force fast-track flight program, Teresa showed up at my parents' house, bawling her eyes out, carrying a pregnancy test."

Without thinking, Rebecca reached across the table and gripped his hand.

"That's not the end of my story, I'm sorry to say. Do you have time for the rest?"

"A few minutes," she said, checking her watch again.

Grant began tying his paper napkin in square knots to keep his hands busy. "I'd only been with Teresa that one night. Naturally I questioned whether I was actually the father. She totally lost it, screaming that she wasn't the type of girl to sleep around. She swore to my parents that she loved me, and thought I loved her. Of course they believed her over me. She had the test as proof."

Grant stuffed the napkin in his cup and scrubbed both hands across his face. "My folks pushed for a wedding. I already knew I had to do the right thing, so I let Mom arrange one at their house. She offered to have Teresa stay with them while I was in San Antonio for my training. I probably should've objected."

"The result was Ryan, I assume."

"No. Our daughter was stillborn at seven months. You'll probably think the worst of me, Rebecca, but in some ways I was relieved. I'd had a taste of flying, and had my career in sight. Still, this was my daughter and I owed Teresa support. I flew home on emergency leave. It felt like visiting a stranger. I didn't love her. But I should never have told her then that I wanted a divorce. I was an insensitive jerk and she certainly let me know that."

"Oh, no. Teresa was grieving."

"I grieved, too, when I arranged to have our baby buried. I took flowers to Rachel's grave whenever I was in Virginia. Teresa never went. Not once. And she never let me forget what a bastard I'd been. I know now it was a mistake, but I wanted to avoid her anger as much as possible. I frequently requested duty assignments abroad."

"I'd feel sorrier, probably, if you hadn't ended up having two more kids."

"I don't blame you for judging me. But I was a faithful husband, although Teresa didn't believe it. Not even after I suggested a second baby might improve our marriage."

"It rarely does," Rebecca murmured, then pushed back her chair and stood.

Grant glanced at his watch. "By my calculations you have three minutes left on your break. Come, I'll walk you back."

Rebecca seemed flustered by the offer and Grant wondered how long it had been since anyone had taken care of *her*. In an obvious attempt to cover her embarrassment, she straightened their chairs, picked up the cups and dropped them in a trash can as they left their table.

Grant had to lengthen his stride to keep up with Rebecca's faster pace. He set a hand lightly on her waist to guide her around a family of four who were strolling leisurely beside the river.

She tensed under his touch and walked even faster.

"Hey, slow down. Where's the fire?" He reached for her left hand, slowing her mad dash. "Ah…may I ask if you're currently seeing anyone? Dating, I mean?" he added, seeing Rebecca's confusion.

"Heavens, no. Working in the salon all day, then waiting tables at night and on weekends doesn't leave time for a social life."

"You work every weekend?"

"Saturdays. I have Sundays off. That's when I do laundry, run errands and catch up on all the other household tasks."

They had reached the Tumbleweed. But before Rebecca could open the door and escape from him, Grant spoke up. "I want to see you again. I could bring lunch to your salon. Tomorrow, or any other day that's convenient."

"Why? Why would you do that?"

"Because...well, because our kids are involved and you object. I'm not sure I do, but I'm willing to talk about it more."

"Even though you don't want to confront Ryan."

"I want his respect. And yours," Grant said pointedly.

Rebecca wavered. She tried to avoid his gaze, but his brilliant blue eyes held hers, until she felt her shoulders relax.

"Is that a yes?" he asked, with a tentative smile.

"It's crazy," she said. "I have no insights. And we've both been hurt before."

"People heal. Do you ever think about that?"

Rebecca lowered her chin. "Lisa and Jordan have been my life," she said softly. "I haven't gone out with anyone since my divorce."

"Listen, I'm only saying I feel something...a spark. I think you feel it, too. Why not see where it leads?"

"I repeat, it's crazy. Say I agree to lunch, maybe the day after tomorrow," she said, scrambling to remember her appointment schedule. "That's not going to change my mind about not wanting my daughter to date your son. That's a whole separate issue, Grant."

"Absolutely. You and I are adults. They're kids." Grant casually leaned against the side of the building.

"You're right about that. But I won't give up trying to convince you to help me." She gave him directions to her salon and they set a time to meet.

"So we're set? I'll bring sandwiches. Is there someplace we can go to eat and talk?" he asked.

"There's a park across the street. It has great paths we can explore." A tiny smile lifted the corners of her lips for just a moment, then she opened the restaurant door. "It's easy to see where Ryan gets his charm. I think I'm more worried about Lisa than ever."

"Don't be. We'll put our heads together and find a solution that will work out for everyone, Becca."

"No one's ever called me Becca. I kind of like it." She brushed two fingers over Grant's jaw.

Before he could react and do what he'd wanted to do since he'd gotten a whiff of her tantalizing perfume earlier that evening, she hurried inside. *Damn.* He wondered just what he'd agreed to do. Grant hoped he hadn't promised to work against his son, not when they so badly needed to find common ground.

LISA GEROUX had set her alarm so she could get up early. She dressed quietly, then filled her backpack with her schoolbooks. She made sure not to let her bedroom door squeak when she opened it. Glancing up and down the hall, she was relieved to see her mother's door stayed closed.

Feeling she owed Jordan an explanation for leaving without him, since they usually rode the school bus together, she slipped silently into his room. His *messy* room. Sheesh, she wasn't a neat freak, but if she didn't break her neck in here it'd be a miracle.

Reaching his side without mishap, she knelt and clapped a hand over her brother's mouth while she shook him awake.

"Mm-mm-mm!" he gurgled, flailing his arms wildly.

"Jordan, hush! It's me." She didn't remove her hand until his eyes focused blearily on her face.

"What the heck are you doing? I thought I was being smothered!"

"Shh, keep your voice down. I don't want to wake Mom. I'm leaving now, so I won't be taking the bus."

"What time is it?" Jordan asked with a massive yawn. He squinted at his bedside clock. "It's 6:00 a.m. Is it even light out?" He peered past her to the window.

"Almost. I'm off to meet Ryan. I'll catch a ride to school with him."

"Mom's going to be so pissed off."

"That's why he can't pick me up here. He's freaked out because his dad showed up at his game. Ryan thinks he's spying on us."

"Sounds more like something Mom would do."

"I know. She's got it in her head that if I have a boyfriend I won't go to college."

"She's probably seen the silly girls at school who throw themselves at jocks. Most couldn't pour water out of a boot if the instructions were printed on the heel. It's the same with the jocks."

"Ryan's not like that. He said he's been looking into colleges for a while now."

"Saying doesn't make it so."

Lisa sprang to her feet. "Now you sound like Mom. I'm out of here."

"Hey," Jordan called after her. "What am I supposed to tell Mom?"

"Whatever! I don't care. She thinks I don't appreciate her saintly dedication to making sure she eats with us twice a day. You know, Dad wouldn't treat us like babies." Lisa wanted to slam Jordan's door, but forced herself to close it quietly.

She did the same with the front door, although she was careful to make sure it locked. She hoped Ryan remembered to pick her up at the convenience store two blocks away. Most of her friends, even kids a lot younger, had their own cell phones. Lisa had never asked for one. But did her mother give her credit for that? No. She acted like she was the only one who made sacrifices.

Lisa reached the store. No Ryan. She used the quarters in her lunch sack to call him from the pay phone. That was another thing. Three out of five days she made her lunch and Jordan's and didn't get any thanks.

"Ryan?" Lisa heard breathing when the ringing stopped, but no one spoke. "It's Lisa."

"What's wrong?"

"Nothing. Aren't we meeting like we said?" This wasn't going as smoothly as she'd hoped. "I'm at the convenience store on South Zarzamora. Two blocks from my house."

"Does your mother know?"

"Why should I tell her?" Lisa asked flippantly. "Anyway, she worked late and won't be up yet. Listen, I'll buy you a couple of doughnuts."

"Uh, Lisa, maybe this isn't such a hot idea. Last night my dad left the phone book open at the page with the restaurant where you work. And he went out for a while but didn't tell us where he was going."

"Do you think he went there?"

"I'm not sure. Brandy said he acted funny when he saw us together at the game. I don't want to cause trouble for you or your mom."

"I'll have to walk to school if you don't pick me up. I thought we had this planned."

"Okay, Lisa. Jeez. Traffic is crazy this time of the morning and there's no sidewalk along that street. Give me fifteen minutes. I'll be there."

"Thanks," she said, and felt the knot in her stomach begin to uncoil.

Ryan had already showered and dressed. He needed to get a head start on an English paper, but now he tossed his books into a duffel bag with his baseball gear.

He pressed an ear to his father's bedroom door to check if the colonel was up or not. Ryan would rather not get caught on his way out to meet Lisa.

In Germany, he hadn't had to deal with his father wanting to know what he did with his time. Now, the colonel asked dumb stuff, like how were Ryan's classes? Was there anyone he needed to talk to at the high school? This was a new development, and Ryan bristled over the colonel's sudden need to micromanage his life. Ryan and a counselor had looked over his records from Ramstein. They'd chosen classes suited for a college track. As for baseball, he didn't give a damn if his father came to any games. He never had in Germany or anywhere else. What the colonel didn't understand was that he didn't automatically get to be a dad, just because he had decided to retire and work from home.

Ryan grabbed his car keys from the peg the colonel had installed in the kitchen. Another rule. Ryan was supposed to get in the habit of hanging up his keys whenever he was in quarters. It was just one more belated attempt by his old man to take control. *A real pain in the butt.*

He started to leave by the side door, then his conscience kicked in. Ryan waffled but turned back to scribble a note that said: "Went to school early to study with a friend." He signed it with one big *R*.

Pulling his Mustang out of the driveway, Ryan rotated his shoulders to ease the tension.

He found Lisa right where she said she'd be— leaning against the outer wall of the convenience store, drinking a diet soda.

"Is that your breakfast?" He got out and opened the passenger door for her.

She settled into the seat, waiting for him to climb in before she responded. "I thought I'd better buy something since I was hanging around. Remember, I promised I'd buy you breakfast. The doughnut shop on Commerce is closest."

"Let's go to a restaurant that serves real food. I don't do sugar in the morning, or I'll be wired by noon."

Lisa's face fell. "I…ah…don't have that much cash on me."

"My treat," he said causally. "I figured that since you and your mom both work two jobs, money's kind of tight for you."

"Don't remind me. Her two jobs are the reason Jordan and I can't let *anything* deter us from getting good grades and college scholarships. And that includes you, Ryan."

"Parents are weird. They get hung up on stupid stuff," he said, pulling into the parking lot of the first pancake restaurant he saw.

"Your dad seems normal. I mean, you get to have

a social life. And this car. Plus, you said he'll pay for your college."

Ryan didn't comment until after they were seated in a booth and had menus. "Aren't dads supposed to provide for their kids?"

"Mine doesn't," Lisa said, closing her menu.

"I thought he died. Like my mom."

"No. Well, maybe. He and Mom divorced before Jordan was born. I don't know much about him. I was two when we moved here. Jordan and I don't ask about him anymore. Mom always got that look, and changed the subject."

"It's the same at my house, if I ever mention my mom. Her name was Teresa. I was in first grade when she got a bad infection after Brandy was born. She never came home from the hospital."

"That's so sad, Ryan." Lisa broke off when the waitress came to take their order. Ryan asked for bacon and eggs. Lisa said she didn't want anything.

"Bring her the same as me," Ryan said.

The waitress nodded, then left. Ryan studied Lisa across the table. "If you were home what would you eat?"

"Whatever gets fixed. Frozen waffles or corn-flakes if it's my turn to cook. Jordan likes making bacon or ham, and hash browns. Eggs and pancakes or toast if Mom's scheduled."

"You have a schedule?"

"Yeah. For supper, too. Who cooks at your house?"

"Nobody, really. Mostly we do takeout. None of

us can cook. In Germany, the colonel mostly ate on base or in mess kitchens if he was deployed. At the house we had a housekeeper, a cook and a nanny for Brandy."

"You lucky duck."

"Yeah, right," Ryan said, pausing as the waitress set their plates in front of them. "The colonel should've transferred stateside after Mom died. But his commander asked him to stay with the U.S. European Command Post, so he hired staff for us. None of them spoke much English. I knew just enough to figure out that the first housekeeper didn't like kids. And the nanny found ways to communicate everything I did wrong to the colonel."

"Do you always call your father by his rank?"

"He thinks I shouldn't now that he's retired." Ryan shrugged. "He was never really part of my life—more like a distant uncle than a father. Now he wants to be involved. Brandy likes it, but it's a little late for me to get all warm and fuzzy."

"Gee, your folks didn't divorce and you've still got issues. I wonder why anyone gets married and has kids if they're going to do such a crappy job of raising them."

"My mom and dad should've divorced. When I was little they didn't get along. For a kid, I understood a lot. She had him followed, to try and catch him with women."

Lisa stopped eating her eggs. "Did he have, like, a mistress?"

"I don't think so. One time when I was pissed at him, I told him what Mom said. He acted all shocked and said it was ridiculous. He claimed Mom was insecure. My best friend said his mom cried because his dad was gone so much. I guess that could've been Mom's problem. But I doubt it. She wasn't happy even when he was around."

"Maybe she was depressed. My mom gets that way when a lot of things go wrong, like with the house or the car. She has to handle everything alone. If your dad was off with the air force, maybe your mom thought his job came first."

"Maybe. Brandy had a bunch of nannies who tried to get with the colonel. They thought he was hot. It's the uniform. Some women fall all over a guy in uniform," Ryan said, not bothering to hide his disgust.

"My mom never dates. Does your dad?"

Ryan shrugged and drained his coffee. "He wouldn't tell me if he did. You know, I wish he *would* get married. Then he'd quit trying to play superdad. I can take care of myself."

"I wouldn't want a stepparent. Lots of my friends hate theirs. I'm for sure never getting married. Look at all the problems it causes."

"You say that now, but you'll change your mind."

"No. But I do want to find out why my parents divorced. I'm trying to track down my dad. You know…through the Internet."

"Wow. What if he doesn't want to be found?"

Lisa just blinked.

Ryan stood and grabbed the check when the waitress delivered it. He left enough money on the table to cover the amount, plus a tip. "We should go. The campus parking lot will be open by now."

"Sure." She stood. "You know, Ryan, we have a lot in common."

"You mean, like your mom's on your back, and the colonel's on mine?"

"Yes. I can't even have friends over when Mom's working."

"I don't want to invite anyone over. At least not until the colonel finds something else to occupy his spare time. Even then he'd have to get a sitter for Brandy."

"You should bring her along when we take Darcy's boys for ice cream or pizza after your games."

He shook his head. "Brandy would tell the colonel."

"Bribe her."

"My sister is a motor mouth. A bribe wouldn't work."

"She's a cutie, Ryan. You said she's eleven?" He nodded, and Lisa added, "Darcy's oldest are six and five, and the twins are three. I'm sure they'd all get along."

"Let's keep on as we are, Lisa. I need your help in chemistry and you need mine in calculus. Our families don't need to get involved."

THAT AFTERNOON, Jordan met Lisa taking Darcy's boys to the ball game. "What did you tell Mom this morning?" she asked.

"I said you went to school early to cram for a test."

"I hate sneaking around. I wish Mom would be more reasonable."

"She asked me if you were still hanging with Ryan at school."

"What did you say?"

"That my classes are in a different wing from yours, which is true. But I wouldn't worry. I found out I'm flunking geometry. If I don't pull up my grade before quarterly reports go out, Mom won't be hassling you. She'll be on my case."

"That sucks. Ryan could help you. In Germany he tutored math."

"Yeah. Too bad Mom hates him."

The bell signaling the arrival of buses had Jordan jogging off, leaving Lisa staring glumly after him. Darcy was interviewing permanent sitters again. If she found one, it was going to be harder to meet with Ryan.

After the game that day, Ryan doled out chicken strips, fries and milk to the boys, then turned to Lisa. "Did you see there's a dance at the end of next month? It's on a Saturday night. Will you go with me? Uh, I mean, if you don't have to work? I thought if you had enough notice, maybe you could ask for that night off."

She choked on her milk. "You dance?"

"Well, I'll never win *Dancing with the Stars.* But, yeah, I learned in junior high. Didn't you?"

"Well, yeah." She sorted out a French fry disagreement between the twins. "Oh, Ryan, I'd love to go. Maybe I can trade shifts."

"Cool. The dance is pretty casual. You won't have to, you know, spring for anything formal."

"I still have to get past Mom."

"Do you have to tell her you switched shifts with what's-her-name?"

"Katie. I guess not. If for some reason Mom calls me during what's supposed to be my shift, oh well. It's my life. I shouldn't have to miss school dances just because *she* wasn't allowed to do stuff like that when she was growing up."

"Why wasn't she allowed?"

"Her parents are Mennonite, so there was a lot she couldn't do. Because she left the order, it's like she's dead to them. She didn't tell me, but I read that's what they do. Mom swears our house rules aren't a tenth as strict as what she lived with."

"You'd think she'd want you to do more fun things."

"We get TV and iPods. I wear makeup, which her parents didn't approve of. Mom's animosity toward you is bizarre, Ryan. I never expected it."

"It's not like I'm a Goth or some other kind of freak."

Lisa grabbed his hand. "You're great," she said with feeling. Then he laughed, making her blush. "I am so excited about this dance. I'm going, and that's all there is to it." She opened her day planner and made herself a note.

They settled down to study together until the boys got restless.

Later, Lisa phoned Katie. They agreed to trade days. The fact that it all worked out lessened the disappointment at hearing Darcy had found a new live-in sitter.

CHAPTER FOUR

THE SALON reminded Grant of controlled bedlam when he arrived ten minutes early for his lunch date with Rebecca. A gaggle of women tried to talk over a windy chorus of commercial hair dryers. Rebecca's attention was firmly fixed on her client and she didn't notice him walk in.

She looked at home, he thought. Cute, even amid the gleaming, pink and black surroundings. A black skirt hit her midcalf, and he thought once again that she had very nice legs.

However, there was no denying that the carnation-pink apron she had on clashed horribly with her red curls, feathered around her face today. The woman in the chair talked a mile a minute. Rebecca nodded at intervals, which apparently suited her client. Rebecca's hands were encased in surgical gloves covered in a pale goo. Grant watched her paint sections of the woman's hair with the goo, and then wrap those same sections in strips of aluminum foil. The client was fast resembling an alien.

"Help you, hon?" asked an older beautician who

greeted him at the counter. Her crown of black braids could only be called a work of art.

"I'll, uh, just wait for Rebecca to finish what she's doing."

The woman flipped through an appointment book. "Do you have an appointment? Rebecca doesn't have anyone listed after Adele."

"No. She… We…" Grant stumbled over what to say, and gestured lamely at the door to indicate they were going out. Obviously Rebecca hadn't told her co-workers about their lunch date. And now, Grant wished he'd hung around outside instead of coming in. More so when the woman with the braids hurried to Rebecca's station and made animated gestures toward where he stood looking very out of place among chintz frills.

Rebecca glanced at the poodle-shaped wall clock and excused herself to her client. Her face betraying her panic, she sped over to Grant. "I'm so sorry! I'm running behind. A few clients came late," she babbled, waving the gooey paintbrush. "With the weather so blustery, I wasn't even sure you'd show. Lunch in the park won't be pleasant."

"I'd never cancel without calling, Rebecca. Besides, I've been looking forward to this. One of my neighbors works at the Tower of the Americas in HemisFair Park. When it looked like it might rain today, I asked if he knew a good place to eat in this area. He suggested the restaurant on the top floor of his building. Said it's nice and quiet for lunch or dinner. I made reservations for twelve-thirty. If you need more time, I'll phone and have them change it to one."

"You don't mean the revolving restaurant? Grant..." She struggled to get the words out, and ended fluttering her gloved hands in the air. "I can't go *there*. Grant, that place is way too fancy. I'm not dressed for that today—if ever."

"You look fine to me. Well, I assume you'll ditch the apron thing."

"Smock. Yes, but... Please, I'd feel out of place. Being new in town, you probably don't realize how expensive that restaurant is." She lowered her voice. "I hear they even have a private glass elevator to take customers straight to the top."

"Yes, Harper mentioned that. My neighbor, Harper Douglas. He's a lawyer."

"There you have it. With what lawyers charge, he can afford it. Anyway, I can't take that long a lunch. And now I need to get back to Adele or her champagne streaks will come out too light."

Grant had no idea what champagne streaks were, but he could easily see through the excuse. It was clear Rebecca was trying to back out because he'd unwittingly picked a restaurant that cost more than she deemed appropriate. "I'll cancel the reservation, and wait for you. You choose a place. I don't care if it's a hole in a wall—I came to see you."

The earlier panic returned to her eyes as she looked back and forth between him and her waiting client.

"Really, Rebecca. Take care of your customer. I have no plans other than eating with you."

"I didn't think eating was the main point. We said we'd get together to talk about our kids."

Grant clutched his chest and groaned. "You wound me, Rebecca. Here I thought I'd charmed you over with my wit and charisma."

As if she had no idea how to take his clowning, Rebecca backed away shaking her head.

A steady stream of women came and went from the salon. The rare one paused briefly in the waiting area. None of the fabric-covered chairs allowed Grant to sit where he could continue to watch Rebecca, so he picked up a magazine.

The glossy tabloid gave the lowdown on movie stars. Their stories set him to thinking about the direction people chose for their lives. The stuff a person could control, and crap that fell on them along the way. He thought about his kids, Ryan and Brandy, but also about something Rebecca had said. About wanting so much for her children. She wanted so much more for Lisa and Jordan than she'd had, or currently had. He had spilled his guts over their coffee the other night, but Rebecca had been reserved in what she shared. All she'd said was that they were both wounded.

Grant set the magazine aside, wondering how wounded. For all that he'd gone through with Teresa, he felt mostly unscathed. Other than in his relationship with Ryan.

He drummed his fingers on one knee, mulling over ways to get Rebecca to open up to him, when he noticed she'd finished with her client. Rebecca and the woman stood at the counter, discussing a future appointment. The client paid and swept past Grant, leaving a trail of perfume in her wake.

"Give me a minute to wash the hair spray off my hands, and I'm ready to go. Are you okay with Thai food? It's the nearest place. And they're fast. My next appointment is in half an hour."

Grant hadn't realized their time would be so short.

"It's not okay?" she asked quickly when he hesitated.

"Oh, no. Thai is great." He smiled, not wanting to give Rebecca any reason to skip eating with him altogether. "I half expected local restaurants to serve Mexican, is all," he added. "When I trained at the base years ago, it was hard to find even a hamburger without green chili sauce."

"You'll still find that at the *mercado* over around Market Square. This part of San Antonio changes constantly. One culture moves out and another moves in. Our shop hangs on, but Trudy, the owner, says we may have to find a different location. A lot of stylists used to regularly take clients until nine at night. Not so much now. The area's gotten pretty rough. Clients are afraid of having to walk so far. And since shop owners along both sides of the street live above their businesses, parking gets next to impossible after six. Anyway, you don't care about that, I'm sure. I'll just go wash and be right back."

But Grant discovered he did care. Where would her kids be if something happened to Rebecca?

Intending to ask, he opened the door for her the minute she appeared. Then he was forced to jog to catch up, because she strode quickly up the narrow sidewalk into the wind.

Grant hadn't noticed the run-down condition of the area when he arrived. Weathered brick and adobe buildings, some quite shabby, lined the street. The concrete sidewalk was broken in places and weeds poked through the cracks.

A bell jingled when they entered the restaurant. An older Thai gentleman materialized from behind a painted screen, plucked a couple of menus from the counter and led them to one of only two empty booths. Steam from the kitchen in back wafted through the room. "Smells good," Grant commented. "I didn't realize I was so hungry. What do you recommend?"

Rebecca studied her menu. "I've never eaten here. I always pack my lunch. If I ate out every day it would use up everything I made. But my colleagues say this place serves a lot for a fair price."

"Don't worry about that. This is on me."

"No, it isn't. I can pay for my own lunch," she said stiffly.

"I've no doubt about that." Grant frowned. "I invited you out, Rebecca. I didn't mean it to cost you anything."

Rebecca looked so nervous, Grant had to smile. At the sight of his crooked grin, she seemed to relax. The tension in her jaw and shoulders eased.

The waitress brought a steaming earthenware pot of tea and twin cups. She took their order, then quickly left them to their conversation.

"Lisa went to school before I got up yesterday. I'm hoping you'll tell me that Ryan went at his usual time." She took a sip of tea, as Grant cupped his drink in both hands.

"No, he went early, too. Unusually early, in fact. He put a note on the fridge. Ryan said he was going to study with a group. It's plausible," Grant rushed to say, since Rebecca's scowl had deepened. "Quarterly tests are coming up."

Sounding bleak, Rebecca said, "I know kids today are supposedly defiant. I just haven't experienced it until now."

"I'm not sure going to school early can be called defiant."

"It is if Lisa avoided mentioning it to me."

Grant raised one eyebrow. "Ryan rarely tells me his plans. You must run a tight ship at your house."

"Not compared to how I grew up. Going against my parents' rules wasn't tolerated. Jack and I left the community after we got married, which was considered disobedient. Our families cut us off."

"Where on earth did you grow up? That sounds harsh."

She waved away steam coming out of the teapot

and avoided his eyes. "I was born in Oregon, in a conservative religious order. We were Mennonite."

"That's kind of like Amish, right? Aren't they conscientious objectors?"

"Pacifists, yes. Only some aren't with their own families. Jack's father wasn't just stern, he was cruel. I think that's why Jack was anxious to leave the order as soon as we got married."

"And you went because you were his wife?"

"I briefly attended a public school in Salem. I'd seen how much more there could be to life. I was excited when Jack suggested we go live in Portland." She shrugged, then seemed to withdraw into her thoughts.

Grant nudged her out of her reverie. "What happened? I told you all about my past the other night. I want to know yours, Rebecca."

Their meal arrived and Rebecca turned gratefully to the food, seeming ready to drop the conversation. Grant wanted to hear more about her marriage. He understood her reserved nature a little better now, but couldn't believe that was the end of the story. He was afraid settling down to eat would kill her incentive to continue.

"Did you have an elaborate wedding? I'm already wondering what to expect when my daughter gets married," Grant said. "Of course, Brandy's still a long way from that."

Rebecca laughed. "I guess you could call mine plain. In accordance with our faith, we had no flowers, music or excess of any kind. Jack and I worked right up until the ceremony. He picked peaches and I worked in the canning shed. I remember we both itched like crazy from peach fuzz." She paused a moment, staring into space. "I was happy, though, because we planned to leave that night."

"Did Jack have a car? Or am I confusing them with the Amish? Maybe Mennonites drive."

"Some do. We didn't have a car. I only learned to drive after I moved here, in fact. John, Jack's dad, was even more traditional than my parents and wouldn't allow any modern conveniences. Not Jack. He loved working on engines. He fixed the old farm equipment that was used in our community. A few farmers from the progressive sect had tractors."

She nibbled at a piece of satay chicken, apparently finished reminiscing.

"Don't tell me you hitchhiked to the city on your wedding night."

"We walked into Salem, about five miles. Jack had a few bucks and enough coins for two bus fares. That was when I realized how broke we were. I didn't have a cent. Women didn't in our society. I vowed to change that as soon as I could. We actually slept on a park bench for two nights in Portland. That scared me to death, and drove me to find my first paying job. I was hired as a waitress by a really nice man, a grandfatherly sort. He was so patient when it came to teaching me how to deal with customers.

My wages and tips allowed us to rent a cheap, daily-rate room. We were so naive," she mused.

"What kind of a job did Jack get?" Grant asked, watching Rebecca blindly push her noodles around on her plate.

"Jack tried...for a while." Her eyes glistened and she tried to blot them without Grant noticing. "Jack only had an eighth-grade education. Boys in the order were needed to work the farms and the orchards. Jobs were different in the city. Jack had this dream of fixing cars, but very little experience. None of the auto shops wanted to train him."

"I get a feeling you're defending him."

"No. But some people grow and change, and others don't. We muddled along month after month on what I earned. I studied between shifts and got my GED. I'd always had a hankering to learn, and I read a lot on my own. Then, I heard about an entry-level position at an insurance company not far from the apartment we'd finally rented. The pay was low to start, but I saw an opportunity to move up."

"So Jack didn't work at all?"

"He had a series of manual-labor jobs. Dishwashing wasn't fixing cars. I understood his frustration. That's why I ended up going back to the restaurant to work night shifts. But a second job didn't leave much time to study insurance policies and procedures. I found out newer girls were being promoted over me, because they had college degrees."

"Ah, I'm beginning to see why Lisa's grades are such a big deal to you. Don't get me wrong. I agree that college is important. It's just…well, education is a balance of a lot of things, Rebecca."

"Like what?"

"Travel, sometimes athletics. General life experience. Or it could be getting married and raising a family."

"But wouldn't you agree that there's more security in having a good education? Especially for a girl? What guarantee is there that the man she chooses will be a good partner? And when the marriage fails, then what?"

"You said *when* the marriage fails, Rebecca, not *if* it does. Some marriages have been known to succeed." Grant studied her for a reaction, but her expression remained neutral as she continued eating. "Speaking of *you* now, not Lisa…have you sworn off marriage for good?"

Rebecca helped herself to more noodles instead of answering. Silence lengthened between them. "To be honest," she said, after finishing a mouthful, "I would've considered it more right after my kids started school. I worked two waitressing jobs then. Max, the owner of the Tumbleweed, also has a sports bar across town. They cater more to the drinking crowd. I worked there until I saved enough money for beauty school."

"Do you make more at the salon?"

She wrinkled her nose. "The tips were better at

the sports bar. But at the salon I don't have to deal with drunks."

Grant pushed his plate aside and poured them each another cup of tea. "So why did you divorce, if you don't mind my asking. Were you tired of supporting Jack, too?"

She folded her napkin and set it beside her plate. "Enough about me, Grant. You know, I'm really full. Why don't you take the last two spring rolls."

He helped himself. "About dating…"

Rebecca averted her eyes from his steady gaze. "Surely you can see how impossible dating would be for me. Plus, I don't go anywhere I'd meet men. Beauty salons, at least where I work, don't exactly have a lot hanging around. The Tumbleweed is largely a family restaurant. Guys who come there are either married or they work nearby and are too wrapped up in their BlackBerries and cell phones to look twice at a waitress."

"Believe me, I'd be looking," Grant blurted. "I'll be honest, Rebecca. I've enjoyed spending time with you. I'd like us to go out again. Maybe to dinner and a movie." He pushed his plate aside, took out his wallet and laid a credit card on top of the bill tray.

Rebecca grabbed her purse and opened it, but Grant waved her off. "My treat, remember?"

"Thank you," she said, acting for all the world as if he'd put her in a very uncomfortable spot.

The waitress appeared to collect Grant's credit

card. Left with nothing to do, Rebecca refolded her napkin.

She still hadn't responded to Grant's invitation when they left the restaurant and made the leisurely walk to the salon.

"It can't be as late as I thought," Rebecca said as she glanced in the window. "My client hasn't arrived yet."

"Let's take a walk, then, now that the wind's died down," Grant suggested. "You could show me the park, if you like."

"That would be nice." Rebecca started off.

Grant caught up and settled his hand at her waist. Their shoulders bumped with each step, but neither pulled away.

"Here it is," she said, gesturing to a compact lawn with picnic tables. A stream ran through the greenery, and trees shaded the tables.

"It's charming, Rebecca," he said as she headed uphill again. "I hope you'll agree to see me again. I promise next time I'll bring sandwiches, and we can eat here in the park as planned."

"I'm surprised you'd want to after I bored you at lunch."

Grant held her arm and turned her to face him. "I wasn't bored. I'm impressed by what you've accomplished," he said earnestly.

Reaching up, Rebecca traced a laugh line curving alongside his mouth. "You have a compassionate face. I think you're probably a very kind man."

Grant carried her hand to his lips. As he brushed a kiss over her knuckles, his eyes locked with hers. For a moment, nothing existed other than the two of them.

A car honked, and the silence was broken. Grant said, "I hope you'll be able to trust me. I know we planned to discuss Ryan and Lisa today, but I'm not sorry we talked about you instead."

"I have to go, Grant. My next client just pulled in across the street."

"Can we meet on Friday? I'll pick you up at the salon again." He pulled a business card out of his pocket and wrote down two numbers on the back. "The top one is my home, the lower, my cell. Check your schedule. Call and let me know what time Friday works for you. If you don't phone, Rebecca, I'll be in your waiting room at twelve sharp."

"One o'clock. On Fridays I go from eight to one without breaks. Why don't I bring an extra sandwich for you?" Grant exhaled with relief, grateful that Rebecca was warming to the idea of seeing him again.

"No. Let me bring the food. My daughter is so sure I can't boil water or spread peanut butter on a slice of bread, I need to prove to myself I'm not a total kitchen klutz."

Rebecca's laughter welled up from deep inside and brought back the color that had drained from her cheeks during her storytelling. "All right, but you've got to promise we'll come up with some kind of plan for the kids. Otherwise I can't justify meeting you for lunch, Grant."

That remark dampened his spirits a bit, but he was distracted by the dusting of freckles across her nose. So much so, he had trouble refocusing his thoughts. "I promise," he murmured. "Between now and Friday, I'll figure out how to make peace with Ryan. I don't know why it's so difficult. After all, I was his age once. I should be able to relate to him better."

"I hope so. After all, our kids are the whole reason for us to see each other. Goodbye, Grant. Thanks again for lunch." She hurried into the salon.

As he called out a final goodbye and headed for his car, Grant thought he should've corrected Rebecca's impression. Their kids weren't why he wanted to see her again.

Who would've thought it? Not him. Not before Rebecca engineered their first meeting. Until then, Grant hadn't met any woman he wanted to pursue past a first date. He wasn't going to try to analyze why he felt differently about Rebecca Geroux. He just did.

Looking forward to Friday restored a zing to his life that for too long had been dull.

On the drive home, Grant caught himself whistling.

CHAPTER FIVE

REBECCA SPENT the afternoon chastising herself for agreeing to meet Grant for lunch again. She certainly shouldn't be this excited at the prospect.

The man was Ryan Lane's dad. The same Ryan who was steering Lisa off course. Or maybe not, Rebecca mused later as she drove home. Lisa had always been strong-willed. *Like her.* Ouch, but that was true.

Perhaps her relationship with Grant had started because they were able to bond over having tension at home. Grant had mentioned that he and Ryan weren't getting along. Rebecca recalled small issues a few weeks before Ryan's name came up, flare-ups she'd had with Lisa. Mostly to do with housework. Increasingly, though, Lisa had started asking why Rebecca had left their dad—and blaming her for the divorce. Rebecca supposed it was natural for her daughter to be curious. Even Grant had been.

Her kids were old enough now that they ought to understand if she explained part of the reasons. But facing them, figuring out what to say and what to keep to herself, had always stymied her. Rebecca couldn't imagine sharing more than what she'd told Grant. And he didn't even know the worst of it.

Yes, she thought as she arrived home, it was time to come clean with Lisa and Jordan. Not about all the gritty details, but about some.

Jordan was in the living room when Rebecca walked in. He closed his schoolbook and took the earpiece to his iPod out of his ear. "Before you ask, Lisa's not here. Ryan pitched a no-hitter and he took Lisa and Darcy's kids out for burgers to celebrate."

"Not again." Rebecca set her purse and jacket on the couch next to her son. "I thought Darcy said she'd hired a new sitter."

"I dunno anything about that. I bumped into Ryan getting off the athletic bus. The team played a noon game at another school—I forget which one. He left to find Lisa and I got on my bus."

Hoping Jordan would be more forthcoming than his sister, Rebecca asked a leading question. "Jordan, has Lisa mentioned anything to you about a big date next month?"

Jordan had always been a terrible liar. Just now his guilty expression betrayed him even as he shook his head. *He knows, the stinker.*

"It's my job to keep you guys safe. I worry this so-called big date may involve traveling in cars, and I need to know what's planned so that I can do my job."

"She hasn't told me anything. Ask her, why don't you?"

"Oh, Jordan." Rebecca rubbed her temples. "You've seen how she's been with me lately. Your sister's…well, she's stubborn."

"Mom, I'm not gonna narc on her. Uh, even if I knew anything." He hurriedly attempted to cover his slip of tongue.

Rebecca sighed heavily, but thought back to the times her brother tattled on her.

She and Mark may as well have been born to different parents. She'd written two letters to her family after she and Jack moved to Portland, but both were returned. Mark had slashed a line through her return name and address and scrawled *person unknown.* It still saddened her to think about it.

"Honey, go on back to your homework. Is there anything I can help you with before I head out for my shift at the Tumbleweed?"

Jordan screwed his lips to one side. "How are you at geometry?"

"Sorry. Once you passed simple adding and sub-tracting, multiplying and easy division, you lost me. Lisa should be home soon. Maybe she'll help you."

"I have a different teacher than she had, and we're using a newer book. She tried to help the other night, but finally said she didn't understand the revised concepts. If I'm gonna pass this class, Mom, I'm going to need a tutor. Even Lisa said so."

"Are they expensive? I suppose they charge by the hour." She mentally added the cost to her monthly budget and wondered how she would cover it.

"The office has a list of retired math teachers who'll tutor, but I'm not sure what they charge. I can get help for free, though."

"Free? How?"

"From Ryan. He's a genius at math."

Rebecca's eyebrows shot up. "Says who? Did your sister put you up to this?"

"No, I swear." Jordan raised a hand. "All around school kids say how smart he is because classes in Germany were harder than ours. Mom, you only saw Ryan once for two minutes. Why do you hate him so much?"

"I don't hate him, Jordan. I'm not happy with what's happened to Lisa since she started hanging out with him. Tomorrow I'll phone your geometry teacher and see if he can recommend a good, inexpensive tutor."

Rebecca headed for the kitchen. "Is an omelet and toast okay for supper? I don't have time to prepare anything more complicated. It's supposed to be Lisa's night to cook, but it's been impossible to get her to focus on her chores since she hooked up with Ryan. Now she misses eating evening meals with the family."

The phone rang and Rebecca answered in the kitchen.

"Mom, it's me," Lisa said. "Darcy wonders if I can stay with the boys so she can go grocery shopping without them."

"Lisa, I'm not stupid. You're just looking to spend

more time with Ryan, aren't you?" Rebecca felt herself flush then as she remembered making plans to see Grant again. But that was different, wasn't it?

"I am not, Mom. You're *so* suspicious. Here, talk to Darcy. This is totally unfair."

A loud clack as Lisa apparently banged the receiver down caused Rebecca to jerk the phone away from her ear. She shut her eyes, muttering to herself as she waited for her friend to come on the line.

"Rebecca? Sorry for causing trouble between you two. It's always a challenge to take four boys to the grocery store. I need to stock up on staples because my new live-in sitter starts tomorrow or I'd never ask. I'd hate to have her judge me because there's no food in the house. I can drive Lisa home afterward."

"It's fine, Darce. I shouldn't have jumped to conclusions. I just don't know how to get back on track with that girl."

"Teen years suck. I don't envy you at all. Maybe try recalling how you felt at her age. I'd offer to talk to her, but I'd rather not interfere. I don't want her to be mad at me if this new sitter doesn't work out."

"Of course. I know you can't get involved. We'll talk later. Bye, Darcy." Rebecca hung up feeling as alone as she'd ever felt.

"Are you okay, Mom?" Jordan asked after she called him to the table.

She mustered a smile. "I just spoke to Lisa and Darcy. Darcy needs your sister to watch the boys so she can grocery shop. I hate going off and leaving you by yourself tonight."

"Mom, please. I'll be fine. You worry too much. Lisa reminded me the other day that it won't be long until we're both in college." He prodded his omelet and looked concerned. "What'll you do then?"

Rebecca brightened and said mischievously, "Oh, I don't know. Maybe I'll enroll in college and go with one of you."

"Mom!"

"I'm kidding. Eat up. I have to run or I'll be late."

They didn't talk much during the meal. Rebecca smoothed Jordan's cowlick down before dashing out of the house, giving her usual instructions.

While looking for a parking spot near the restaurant, Rebecca reflected on what Jordan had said. Truthfully she hadn't ever thought about what she'd do once her kids left home. The prospect of having no one around to talk to seemed bleak.

Grant must be going through that to some degree now. She'd have to ask him what he did to fill his days, though. Rebecca doubted she'd ever be able to retire.

Forced to run the two blocks from her car to the Tumbleweed, it crossed her mind that it wouldn't hurt to be a little less busy.

Her first customers were a group of girls who looked to be about Lisa's age. They had menus, but didn't acknowledge her as she walked up. "What can I get you girls to drink?" She finally butted in because other tables were beginning to fill up. They could go back to their conversation while she filled their drink order.

One, a pretty brunette wearing a boy's letterman jacket, appeared annoyed by Rebecca's interruption. Glancing up with a frown, the girl exclaimed, "Aren't you Lisa Geroux's mom? You must think it's the coolest thing ever that Ryan Lane invited *her* to the Spring Fling next month. We all thought—" she included her friends in her statement "—that Lisa was too much of a brainiac to get someone as hot as him."

"Apparently we were wrong," sniffed a made-up blonde seated across from the speaker. "Lately, you never see one without the other."

"Yeah," a third girl, one with green eyes and braces, chimed in. "Did Lisa, like, get a new perfume we don't know about? If so, I hope you share her secret with us, Mrs. Geroux. Or is it Ms.? That's why Lisa has to work, right? Her dad's gone."

The girls pretended to try to smother their laughter. Rebecca whipped her head back to the one who'd started the questioning—the dark-haired ringleader. It didn't take much to see through that snarky little miss and her cohorts. Clearly these girls came here just to mock Lisa and her family. Rebecca had an excellent memory for faces and she couldn't remember ever seeing them at the Tumbleweed before.

Their smug sense of superiority got to Rebecca. She knew what they were trying to do. Their jewelry and purses alone identified them as part of the country-club set—far removed from Lisa's usual circles.

Rebecca opened her pad. "Are you ready to order? Tonight's special is short ribs."

The ringleader got up and signaled her friends. "The other waitress served us water, but water's free, right? We checked your menu. Everything on it is loaded with carbs. We're watching carbs, aren't we, girls? I have to look model perfect for the Spring Fling—once I decide which lucky guy gets to take me." With a toss of her shiny hair, the girl collected her designer purse.

The blonde opened one sack. "Are you sure this dress makes me look like Reese Witherspoon?"

"Absolutely," the third girl vouched. "Come on. I want to go back to Club Monaco to get that skirt," she said, snatching up the last of the boutique sacks piled on the empty chair at their table.

Rebecca began collecting the water glasses, which she almost dropped when the brunette insisted to her friend that at two hundred seventy-five dollars, the skirt was a steal.

Rebecca knew she shouldn't take their bait. She was, after all, the adult. Their snide jabs at Lisa sizzled like fire in the pit of her stomach, but Rebecca held her tongue, knowing that anything she said would only make matters worse for her daughter. Trying not to appear rushed, or angry, she made her way to the kitchen. All the same she stewed over their comments, which those girls had no doubt intended.

Needing to cool off, Rebecca took her time fixing two new pots of coffee.

It was bad enough learning about her daughter's plans secondhand. Discovering what kind of people Lisa had to face at school was heartrending.

Rebecca admitted to feeling hurt that Lisa hadn't confided in her. But what was Lisa thinking—trying to fit in with that crowd?

Rebecca hadn't anticipated anything like this when she'd bought their house. She'd researched where she wanted to raise her children based on the quality of the schools in the area. It'd been a stroke of luck to find an affordable small house in such an affluent district. Lisa had been in fifth grade then, and kids looked like clones in blue jeans. Who would've thought that one day they'd have to contend with dances where sixteen- and seventeen-year-olds wore designer outfits? Not Rebecca. She simply had to make Lisa be realistic.

The kids were both in bed when Rebecca arrived home after her shift. She folded a load of laundry, but still felt anxious about talking to Lisa, knowing it couldn't be avoided for long.

That night her dreams were disjointed. Grant Lane played a part. Tall, handsome and rock-steady, he tried to comfort her after a huge fight with Lisa.

The alarm clock jerked Rebecca out of Grant's

arms. She blinked and glanced around her familiar room, disappointed to find he had only been a dream.

On a brighter note, tomorrow was Friday, and she'd be seeing Grant for real. When she told him what she'd heard from the girls at the restaurant, surely he would agree that their kids had no business going to such an expensive event. She assumed the dance was pricy, given what those girls planned to wear. At least, Ryan was likely to bear much of the cost. She and Grant needed to brainstorm ideas on how to get the kids to realize they couldn't afford it.

At breakfast there was the usual rushing around, setting out lunches, finding books and making sure everything was in backpacks before anyone sat down to eat.

Rebecca handed Lisa a bowl of scrambled eggs and said, "Three girls came into the Tumbleweed last night. They go to your school and were talking about an upcoming dance. I think one girl called it a Spring Fling?" Rebecca made it a question, hoping Lisa would reveal her intentions. Lisa didn't say a word.

Jordan continued buttering his toast.

"My parents didn't believe in dancing," Rebecca said, scooping eggs onto her own plate. "And I was never allowed to listen to music. I loved it when town kids brought their mini radios to school. They played them at lunchtime, and some kids danced.

One girl from town tried to show me a few steps, but I never learned. She said I had two left feet."

Jordan put the lid on the margarine tub, and joined the conversation. "I think I inherited that from you, Mom. We had a dance segment in PE last year and I *always* got stuck with Emily Grover. She told Mr. Drake that I stepped all over her toes."

Rebecca noticed Lisa passed up an opportunity to tease her brother. She ate fast and kept her eyes trained on her plate.

Trying another tack, Rebecca said pleasantly, "Well, these girls were certainly excited. And they had clothing bags galore. I'm glad neither of you are going. I can't afford to dress you like those kids— never mind the cost of the tickets."

"May I be excused?" Lisa was already on her feet, carrying her plate to the sink. "I'm going to go brush my teeth, Jordan. I'll meet you at the bus stop, okay?"

Bobbing his head, Jordan gobbled his toast and drained his juice.

So much for subtlety. Rebecca debated saying straight out what the girls at the Tumbleweed had said about Lisa and Ryan, but refrained. Her worried expression must have alerted Jordan. As he deposited his dishes in the sink, he said, "Mom, don't ask me anything. I'm not gonna snitch."

"I'm not asking," Rebecca murmured. "I never liked it when my parents had your uncle Mark spy on me and report back to them. I wish he'd defended me the way you defend Lisa."

"I have an uncle?" Jordan's brow furrowed.

"Had. I haven't seen any of my family since your father and I were shunned for moving away. It's complicated, but leaving our church order was the same as if we'd died."

"Did your brother spy on you and Dad when you dated?"

"We never really dated like secular people do. He brought lugs of fruit in from the fields, and I worked in the sheds making apple butter, or canning other fruit to sell at our roadside stands. Our courtship was pretty much just flirting."

"Huh. After you got divorced, did he go back to the order?"

"No. Jordan, this is a conversation we need to have as a family. Not now—Lisa's already gone, and you're about to miss your bus. Our lives growing up were so different from anything you and Lisa know there isn't time to get into it. We'll discuss it together someday, but not while your sister's in a snit."

"She's always in a snit."

"Hopefully, that, too, will pass, Jordan. I promise we'll talk before she goes to college."

"Holy cow! That's not for two years."

"A year and a half. Surely by then, she'll be over this rebelliousness and back to her old self."

Jordan grabbed his backpack. "I'm not holding

my breath," he said, sounding peeved. He hurried out of the room without looking back.

Rebecca didn't have time to dawdle. She loaded the dishwasher and finished dressing for work. Plus, she still had to figure out what to do about her broken disposal. The noxious odor was becoming harder to ignore. Fixing it probably wasn't an option. They needed a new one.

Over her lunch break, Rebecca crunched budget numbers. Next month, barring any emergencies, she should be able to swing the replacement costs. She penciled her budget book.

Things got crazy in the afternoon. She took a late walk-in customer, and, as a result, had to call the kids to say she wouldn't be home for supper. That got a rise out of Lisa and caused another spat. But it couldn't be helped. It paid one more bill. She went straight to the Tumbleweed from the salon.

"Darcy, how's it going?"

"Terrible. The twins hate their new sitter, so they're being pains in the you know what. They want Lisa back. Leaving them tonight wasn't pretty. And if you want to know the truth, I don't know about this woman. She acted like I shouldn't leave when the boys were throwing tantrums. So…how are things with you?"

"Not good. Lisa's being a bit of a pain herself. It all has to do with that boy I told you about, Ryan Lane."

"I meant to ask you how it went with his father, Mr. Dreamy."

Rebecca felt her face heat. "His name is Grant. Actually, he's…nice. He took me out for lunch the other day. He…ah…is bringing lunch tomorrow, too. We're going to eat in the park."

Darcy whistled through her teeth. "This is huge. Shoot, there's my order. Hold that thought—I want to hear more." She grinned at Rebecca's sputtering, then darted off to deliver her orders.

The restaurant filled up, and the friends never had a minute to talk again. It was Darcy's night to close, so Rebecca happily skipped out at the end of her shift. She didn't know how much she wanted to share about her time with Grant. She could shrug and say there wasn't anything going on. But she knew Darcy would see right through her.

AT THE SALON on Friday, the closer it got to noon, the more frequently Rebecca checked the clock, and the more nervous she became. Jeez, when had she become this giddy adolescent? She was no better than Lisa!

Grant walked in as Rebecca said goodbye to her last morning customer. She knew she flushed all over the instant she saw him. His smile lit a fire inside her.

He held up a wicker basket covered over with a red-and-white-checked cloth as he approached her. "I came to steal you away for a picnic as promised."

Rebecca struggled to sound calm. "I haven't been on a picnic in years. When the kids were little, I'd pack a lunch and take them to the park when I managed to get an afternoon off. I saw people with wicker baskets and thought that was so cool."

"I'm glad you like it. I know it's a cliché, but I thought it was fun. Are you ready to go?"

She stripped off her work smock and left it at her station. That giddy feeling returned, washing away her cares, but leaving a vague sense of guilt. She was, after all, doing something she had forbidden daughter to do, wasting time with a man.

Grant casually twined the fingers of his free hand with Rebecca's. She felt years younger and some of the guilt eased.

"How have you been?" she asked, then worried that she was too formal. Her heart fluttered and she hoped he couldn't feel her nervousness.

"I probably shouldn't admit that I've mostly been counting the days until I could see you again," he said sheepishly.

"You have? Me, too." She missed a step in her eagerness.

Grant caught her before she could fall. "That's nice. Very nice," he repeated, smiling into her eyes. "I was afraid you'd have second thoughts."

She shrugged. "I had second, third and fourth thoughts. I don't understand it, but I can't seem to talk myself out of wanting to see you."

"Good. Don't try. Accept that when attraction strikes, it strikes."

"What if I said I wasn't attracted to you?"

Laughing, Grant squeezed her hand. "I wouldn't believe you. I felt something when we met for coffee. And you must've, too. Even as mad as you got, you didn't pour any hot coffee over my head."

She leaned into him. "I did come on a bit strong, didn't I?"

"I rather liked that about you. Now, we have the park to ourselves. Do you want to grab a table in the shade, or shall we cross the footbridge?"

"Let's cross. Most people tend to stay on this side of the creek, so we'll have more privacy over there." Rebecca chose a table near the stream where they could hear the water splash over the rocks.

Grant removed the cloth from the basket and spread it on the tabletop. "Okay, this is where I make my big confession. I didn't make this lunch. I passed a German deli the other day, and stopped in to see what they had. Well, you tell me if this isn't the best bratwurst and potato salad you've ever eaten." He pulled neat plastic containers from the depths of the basket, each offering a different delicacy.

It was Rebecca's turn to laugh. "You brought enough to serve your family and mine."

"What can I say? We got started talking about Germany, and before I knew it, they convinced me to try a little of everything. But it's okay. Ryan will devour any leftovers I bring home."

"Speaking of Ryan—well, Ryan and Lisa—I found out their big date is a school dance."

"Did Lisa tell you?"

"Are you kidding? I couldn't get a word out of her. A group of her classmates told me at the restaurant—and then I heard them discussing the expensive outfits they planned to wear. You said you'd talk to Ryan about it. Did you?"

"No. I waited to see if he would bring it up on his own. He didn't. But a school dance seems tame, Becca. Where's the harm in that?" Grant stopped spreading mustard on thick slices of brown bread.

"Harm is relative. Those girls were buying designer clothes. One girl thought another got a steal paying almost three hundred dollars for a skirt. One skirt," Rebecca huffed. She reached for a bottle of water, noticing that it was the fancy, fruity-tasting kind. "Why am I talking to you about this when you pay how much for water?"

Grant shrugged. "Girls' clothes cost more than boys' stuff. Brandy wants everything to match. I took her school-shopping myself this year. Her nanny used to take her in Germany. I rarely paid attention to the prices back then. This year was definitely educational." Grant rolled his eyes. "She could've shelled out that much on a skirt without even blinking. I was more concerned with them not being too short."

"How old is your daughter?" Rebecca paused as she scooped out sauerkraut.

"She's eleven. A fifth-grader. What she wants more than anything now is a clarinet. I went to two music stores, but one clarinet looks just like another. Did your kids ever play? Do you have any idea what brand is best?"

"The school loaned Lisa a flute in the fourth grade. She only played one year and lost interest. Could Brandy borrow one that way?"

"She doesn't want to get some other kid's germs in her mouth."

"I'm sure they sterilize the mouthpiece. If you buy new, that's a lot of money wasted if she decides to quit, Grant."

"There are worse things to spend it on."

"Yes, like a skirt, for instance. I can't believe you'd pay three hundred dollars for one item for an eleven-year-old. Do you know how fast kids grow?"

"What's the big deal if it makes her happy?"

"But what does she learn from that? If everything comes so easily, how will she know what's really important? The garbage disposal I need doesn't cost that much, for goodness' sake!"

"I'd be glad to pick up and install a disposal for you, Rebecca."

"Don't be ridiculous. You can't spend that much on me. I'll get a disposal once I can save up enough. Anyway, let's not spend our lunch hour arguing. This is great bratwurst," she said, changing the subject as she cut another slice.

From there, the conversation stayed light, and the time slipped away. Suddenly, Rebecca gave a start. "Heavens, I had no idea it was so late. I have an appointment in fifteen minutes. Grant, this was such a nice break. I can't thank you enough. But we barely made a dent in the food. I hope your kids do eat it," she said, beginning to pack up.

Grant had been sitting right next to her on the bench. He liked the way their arms brushed as they both stood to put the leftovers away. "Your lunch break is too short," he groused. "Tomorrow's Saturday. Can we get together then? We could learn about clarinets."

"I'm sorry, Grant. Saturdays are crazy at the salon. I have standing appointments and can't get away. Plus I work a double shift at the Tumbleweed."

"How about a midnight movie, then?" He stored the containers in the basket, and left Rebecca to fold the tablecloth to fit over top. "Or, if your kids sleep late on Saturday mornings like mine do, maybe we could grab breakfast."

"I really don't think I have any free time," she said, consulting her pocket planner. "You won't believe this, but I haven't been to a movie theater in years. Do they really have shows at midnight?"

"They do," Grant attested. "I'd happily meet you when you get off work at the Tumbleweed."

"Right, and what if my kids wake up and realize I haven't come home?"

"Do they do that often? Mine are always out for the night."

"I guess mine are, too. Okay. Let's make it to-morrow night."

"It's a date."

THEY MET the next evening on the dot of midnight. Grant already had the tickets in hand. "I bought them online," he said when Rebecca asked how he'd gotten them.

"I don't know the first thing about computers," she murmured as they entered the dark theater some fifteen minutes later. As soon as they were seated, Grant put his arm around her.

"Are you okay?" he whispered. "You seem jittery."

"The guilt's getting to me," she whispered. "We never decided what to do about our kids, and here we are sneaking around, going out."

"It's completely different. You and I are adults and should be able to do what we want. Anyway, they only meet at ball games and during the day at fast-food joints."

"Maybe. The hours they do spend together aren't improving Lisa's grades."

"Ryan's smart. I'll see if I can find a way to suggest he help Lisa bring up her grades."

That reassured Rebecca enough that she snuggled against Grant and enjoyed the love story before them. When it was over and everyone filed out, she turned to Grant. "That was a beautiful tear-jerker. I can't believe you chose it."

"I have to say it gave me ideas." Grant grinned as he walked her to her car, keeping one arm around her.

Rebecca didn't say anything.

"This worked out well, I think," he said to prompt her. "Let's do it again soon."

"I enjoyed our evening very much, Grant." Rebecca realized she wasn't used to such attentiveness as they reached her Nissan. It was nice, but left her feeling more helpless than she liked.

"Will you go out to dinner with me?"

"Tonight?" She looked startled.

"Next Saturday. Brandy has a sleepover at a friend's, and Ryan's old enough to stay alone. We'll go to a nice, romantic restaurant, say, with candles and piano music. It'll be great, Becca. Something you won't mind skipping work for."

Rebecca knew she shouldn't consider it. But Grant stirred something inside her. She found him difficult to resist. "I never skip out on work," she finally said. "Even though your idea is tempting."

He kissed her. His lips were warm. Her knees quivered and Rebecca felt her resolve slip further. "*You're* tempting," she murmured after Grant eased away from her. She pressed one hand to the front of his shirt. "Next Saturday? Okay, but let's make it a less fancy restaurant," she said, forcing herself to get a grip again.

"Nope. I intend to wow you."

"We can't meet at my house. Grant, our lives, well, mine, is too complicated. I can't go out dressed in what I wear to work, but if I go home to change my kids will want to know what's up."

"Where there's a will there's a way," he said, bringing her fingers to his lips. "Top hotels have the type of restaurant I want to take you to. Can you put your clothes in a bag and take them to the salon? I'll book a room at the hotel where you can change before dinner. Afterward, you can change back into your work outfit and your kids will never know." He named a hotel near the heart of downtown San Antonio. It was probably the priciest in town.

"That's too much, Grant. I'll just change at the salon and meet you at the hotel at, say, eight o'clock?"

"Eight's perfect. Now, since it's so late, would you like me to follow you home to make sure you get there safely?"

"That's sweet, but I'll be fine. When we do banquets at the Tumbleweed, they can last just as late as this. I'm quite capable, you know."

"Yes, but humor me and lock your doors anyway, okay?" He gave her a final, lingering kiss, then stepped away and closed her door after she'd slipped inside. He stood and watched her drive away.

Rebecca hadn't gone a block before she wished she could take back her promise of another date. This wasn't like her. To miss work—what was she thinking? *That you'd like to know what normal single women do for a change.*

Those thoughts calmed her for a while. But a few days later, Rebecca gave in to her nerves. She phoned Grant on Wednesday, and the minute he answered his phone, she blurted, "I can't go out with you on Saturday. I feel too guilty. What if someone sees us together, and our kids find out? It's too risky."

"The odds of running into anyone we know are

minimal. Besides, I don't care who sees us, Rebecca. But if you're really worried, we can be discreet. Trust me. I'll figure out a way. Say you won't cancel."

"I want to go. I've already requested the night off. Yes. Yes, I'll let you handle it, Grant."

SATURDAY, Rebecca made sure she was the last person in the salon. She owned one decent black dress, and it would have to do. Her heels were so old they were back in style. Since she rarely wore them, they looked brand-new.

Driving to the hotel where she'd agreed to meet Grant, she was nervous as a tick on a hot skillet. He was waiting in the lobby, just as he'd said.

"You look wonderful," he said.

She managed a smile. "I feel like Cinderella, minus the glass slippers and ball gown." She gripped her purse in both hands. "This lobby is intimidating," she said, keeping her voice low. "I've never seen anything so luxurious. What if they decide we don't fit in and they kick us out? Not you. You look…fantastically handsome."

Grant took her hand. "Relax, Rebecca. Follow me. I promised you privacy and you've got it. I booked a room with a balcony, and dinner will be served there. I've already been up and we have a great view of the city."

They were at the elevator, and Rebecca was grateful no one was inside to see her stumble. "You did what?" she exclaimed. "Grant, why on earth…?

That must have cost a small fortune. I can't let you—"

The doors closed them inside the car, and Grant cut her off with a kiss that lasted until the elevator stopped on their floor. By then, Rebecca's head was spinning from the kiss and her knees felt weak.

"This way," Grant said, leading her out of the elevator. "If I remember how the fairytale goes, Cinderella enjoyed every minute of her night out."

"You're very persuasive." Rebecca ran two shaky fingers over his lips, and he kissed her again.

"Grant, what are we doing?" she asked after he broke the kiss and walked her along a deeply carpeted hall to a door he opened with a key card.

"I hope we're getting to know one another better. It's been a long week since I last saw you, Becca."

His earnestness moved Rebecca. A thrill ran through her, and she couldn't remember the last time she'd felt this way. Softening, she brushed aside concerns for the money Grant had spent, and vowed to savor the romantic gesture. This was a night that dreams were made of.

CHAPTER SIX

GRANT HELD the door and let Rebecca enter the gold-and-white room ahead of him. She stopped dead as her eyes lit on the massive king-size bed covered in gold satin. The piles of artfully arranged pillows looked too perfect to disturb. Just beyond the bed was an even more elegant sitting room.

Grant took her purse and her wrap from her cold hands and set them on a couch. "Good, the table's already set. Now, all we have to do is call down our order. They've left menus if you'd like to take a look."

"Do people really live like this?" Rebecca asked as they made their way through the sliding-glass doors at the end of the sitting room to the private balcony. A candlelit table had been set for two. Gold-rimmed Alabaster china gleamed in the flickering light. A bottle of champagne chilled in a stand beside the table.

Stepping up behind Rebecca, Grant handed her the menu and gave her a kiss on the back of her neck. "Would you care for a drink while you look over the selections?"

"Maybe just a taste. I have to drive home later."

Grant paused with the bottle over one glass. "Surely a glass with dinner will be all right."

"I'm not much of a drinker. I have bad memories of the one time I indulged."

Nodding, Grant poured a small amount into both glasses. Passing her one flute, he paused for a toast. "To us. And to better memories."

They drank, but Rebecca choked as she looked at the menu. "Grant, there aren't any prices on this menu. How do we know what to order?"

He trailed a finger over her cheekbone. "Tonight is for magic, Rebecca. Not for questions and worry."

"It does feel magical here." She set down her flute and stepped to the wrought-iron balustrade. "I have yellow orchids on the table, the city at my feet and stars overhead. Before I turn into a pumpkin, I think I'll order the chicken cordon bleu."

Grant laughed heartily, and went inside to place their order. Joining her at the ornate railing a minute later, he said, "It wasn't Cinderella who turned into the pumpkin. She was beautiful with or without the fancy trappings. You are, too, Rebecca."

She rose onto her tiptoes and gave him a kiss that left their hearts racing. "That's for not making what you said sound like false flattery."

"I'm the one who's flattered. You gave up a night's pay to be here with me. I know how extraordinary that is." He slid an arm around her waist. Rebecca relaxed and laid her head against his wide shoulder.

For a few minutes they enjoyed the twinkling stars and the city lights in silence. Grant was first to speak. "I wish we didn't have to talk about our kids, but I think we should get it out of the way. I don't want it standing between us. I've had a week with little to do but think about you and us and them. Well, I did buy Brandy a clarinet. I'm already hoping she'll give it up. I don't know if I'll survive a year of her playing off-key and Ryan yelling at her to stop the noise."

Rebecca raised her head and smiled. "Welcome to the world of single parents, Grant."

"Thanks. I know you think I'm a pushover when it comes to my kids. And that I've been too easy on Ryan when it comes to his relationship with Lisa. But I don't want him getting in over his head, either. I asked him about the dance yesterday."

"Really? And…?" Rebecca held her breath.

"It's the athletic department's yearly fund-raiser. It's being held at the school. I got the impression that the guys from the baseball team and a group of girls are going together. Ryan said the dress code is casual, so that's one thing you won't have to worry about."

"The girls who came to the restaurant didn't seem to think it was all that casual."

"Well, I can't speak for them. But Ryan said he was surprised that one of his friends is getting his date a hibiscus to wear in her hair. Ryan wasn't sure if he was supposed to get something for Lisa. I suggested a simple wrist corsage."

Rebecca turned and lightly touched the petals of the yellow orchids in the center of the table. "If he's giving Lisa flowers, that's pretty serious."

Grant decided not to tell Rebecca about the lecture he'd launched into on birds, bees and responsibilities, or that Ryan had said Grant didn't know him well enough to have that discussion. He'd broken through Ryan's embarrassment and they'd had a decent chat.

"If it makes you feel any better, I learned that none of the ball players drink alcohol, and Ryan likes Lisa for her brains and levelheadedness. He said they do study together, and talk about college. It's almost as though they're friends more than anything." Grant didn't add that Ryan believed Rebecca was too hard on her daughter. That would serve no purpose.

"I talked to Lisa's school counselor again. Lisa's turned in extra-credit work and brought her grades up."

"See? Things are improving. Maybe Ryan's a good influence."

"Maybe." Rebecca looked ready to say more, but was interrupted by two waiters bringing their food.

Their meals looked and smelled terrific. One waiter pulled out Rebecca's chair, then placed her linen napkin across her lap, adding to the surreal feeling of the night. Discussing their children no longer seemed appropriate. The waiters quietly withdrew, leaving Grant and Rebecca alone under a canopy of stars.

They held hands across the table, and spoke of inconsequential things. Grant offered her a bite of his steak au poivre.

"Too peppery," she said, making a face. "I'll keep my chicken, thank you very much. This is such a treat. I've thought about making it at home, but then I figured I could feed all of us for two days on what one stuffed chicken breast costs."

"Rebecca, I'm sorry you have to work so hard. I wish you didn't."

She waved her hand impatiently. "I don't mind too much. Besides, there's really no other option. I just don't like how it affects my kids."

"Not that it's any of my business, but why doesn't your ex pay child support?"

"I don't want anything from Jack," she said fiercely. "Ever!"

He arched one eyebrow. "That's plain enough. More champagne?" Grant gestured to the bottle.

"Water is fine."

"I'm sorry if I upset you. I know it's not easy talking about a rocky marriage. I often wonder how Teresa and I would've ended up if she hadn't died," he mused.

"I thought you patched things up by then. I mean, wasn't it right after Brandy was born?"

"Teresa wasn't fond of Germany. She loved living in California. She hated having me gone. My job took me to hot spots all over the globe. I was a part-time husband. And a part-time dad."

"It must have been hard on you, too."

"Harder on the family." He poured himself more champagne and took a sip. "We were both thrilled to find out we were going to have another daughter. Unfortunately, I had to lead a squadron to Kuwait. I left Teresa pregnant and Ryan starting second grade. It wasn't an easy pregnancy. Teresa was hospitalized in her seventh month, and I managed to fly in overnight. She begged me to stay but I couldn't. Her condition went downhill. They released her, and I thought everything was fine. Until I was abruptly called home from strategy meetings in Qatar because she had to have an emergency C-section."

Rebecca murmured sympathetically, too aware of what came next.

"The doctor had already delivered Brandy by the time I caught a flight out. It was touch and go for her for a while, but she pulled through. Teresa got some kind of infection, and…they couldn't save her."

Rebecca realized that in a way she and Grant were kindred spirits. She felt a fresh wave of empathy. "I think I can understand some of what you went through. We both were single parents with new babies. Other parents have no idea what that emotional roller coaster is like. Juggling work with night feedings and colic."

"You had it rougher. My commanding officer's wife had lists of housekeepers and nannies who knew way more about child care than I did. I thought I was giving my kids the best shot."

"I hear a *but* in that statement."

"Yeah. Ryan thinks I'm a terrible dad. And I'll admit I let my career come first. Until my second tour in Iraq when my plane got shot to hell. I realized that if I died my kids would have to go to my parents or Teresa's mother. None of them are getting any younger. I decided to retire to San Antonio so I could spend more time with my kids. I remembered liking my flight training here. Now that I've met you, Rebecca, I'm positive I couldn't have chosen better."

Flustered by his serious expression, Rebecca felt her palm go damp in his hand.

Grant rose, and Rebecca went willingly into his arms. She felt each button on his shirt and the hard outline of his belt buckle. Her imagination went wild, spreading heat through her body. Dizzy, her first coherent thought was that Lisa would never believe she could have such steamy thoughts.

"Rebecca?" The unspoken question was there in Grant's none-too-steady voice.

She was first to glance toward the shadowy outline of the bed. Her answer was trapped in her throat. Tilting her face up, she met Grant's smoldering gaze.

Understanding flickered in his eyes. "That's not why I booked this room, Rebecca. I only wanted to give you the privacy you seemed to want for dinner."

She exhaled gently. He was leaving the decision up to her. Her answer should have been an unequivocal no but the clear yes she spoke didn't surprise her.

Grant's hot kiss drove any lingering doubt from her mind.

"I want this to be good for you," he said against her hair as they made their way to the bedroom.

Rebecca gripped his arm. "I haven't…not since… What if you're disappointed?"

Gathering her close, he whispered reassuringly in her ear.

"Yes," she said again, and locked her arms around his neck.

Grant had a condom in his wallet. It was a habit drilled into all service personnel starting in basic training.

"Becca…" Grant paused to get control of his voice. "I want you to know you can tell me to stop anytime. I'd hate for you to regret this."

"I'm not backing out, Grant. This is what I want." She pressed a soft, warm kiss to his lips that was almost Grant's undoing. He clasped her around the waist and returned it with an intensity that left them both breathless.

They fell together across the big, fluffy bed. Rebecca kicked off her shoes, then sat up. "We need to do something with this comforter. I'd die if we ruined it."

Grant teased her about being practical, but he tossed aside the mountain of pillows and stripped off the gold comforter. "Try it now," he said, tugging her down beside him. Grant let his hands roam from her wrists to her shoulders and back to her fingertips.

She shivered. "I've been dreaming about making love lately. The man is always you, Grant."

"Oh, sweetheart. Nothing like giving a guy performance anxiety." He laughed lightly when she bit her upper lip and looked worried.

"It's okay." He ran one finger along her jawline to the small cleft in her chin.

"Are you comfortable? Are you sure about this?" he asked.

Rebecca nodded, and he began to undress her. He knew it wasn't going to take him long to reach the boiling point.

"Your skin is so smooth," he said.

"Liar," she said with a smile. "Look, calluses. I don't have a lot of time to pamper my skin."

"I think you're beautiful as you are." Grant stripped off his shirt. Rebecca watched his pants join it on the floor. Her eyes widened when he fumbled for his wallet and pulled out a small foil packet.

"Protection," he said simply. Very soon his breathing grew erratic as he lowered the zipper on her dress, and caressed her bare skin.

She traced her thumbs along his collarbones. He hardened at her touch, and wedged a space between them, knowing otherwise he wouldn't last long enough to make it good for her.

He shouldn't have worried. Rebecca was a warm and willing partner.

After a few moments, he broke their kiss and began to play with a lock of red hair curling around her ear. "Have I told you I like your hair? It's the first thing I noticed about you. You're quite magnificent when you go to bat for someone you love."

"Mennonite girls aren't allowed to ever cut their hair. I wore mine in a single braid until…" Rebecca let the thought trail off, and stretched up for another kiss.

"Remember, nothing counts for us except tonight," Grant said fiercely, kissing his way from her lips to her bra. He soon added that to the growing heap of clothing on the floor.

"You have a few scars, Grant. I feel them on your right side."

"Shrapnel," he said. "From the rocket-propelled grenade I took flying the general of my squadron and some dignitaries to the Baghdad airport. I got us there, but I think we all heard the angels singing. After that flight, both the general and I retired."

She smoothed a hand over the area of pock-marked flesh. "I'm grateful the angels kept you safe for me."

Grant's mouth devoured hers, and soon they were both driven by their need. Rebecca matched his passion with her own. And helped him remove her underwear.

The last thing he dropped was the condom wrapper. Other things held their attention then, like her moans when Grant smoothed the puckered flesh of her nipples with his tongue.

He loved the feel of her work-worn palms grazing his own nipples.

"Thank you for taking care of me," she murmured.

Grant nipped his way down one thigh and back up the other, leaving Rebecca breathless and begging for— "More," she said aloud.

That was what he'd been waiting to hear, why he'd held back as long as he had. Because this was going to be good for Rebecca. The very best.

Grant was grateful for her responsiveness. Grateful they hadn't let the situation with their kids come between them. As he brought them both to climax, he let himself believe that no other barriers would stand in the way of them being together.

Rebecca arched her back in anticipation. Grant obliged by straddling her hips, and his arms quivered as he slowly entered her.

She cried out. He stopped at once, afraid he'd hurt her.

"No, no, don't stop." She held him tighter.

That was all the encouragement Grant needed. But rather than press her into the mattress, he flipped their positions, leaving her in command. Her eyes opened in surprise.

Leaning up on his elbows, Grant urged her mouth down to meet his kiss.

A last burst of energy had them collapsing together very near the edge of the bed.

"Don't move," Grant warned lazily. "Or we're likely to fall on the floor."

"I couldn't move if my life depended on it." Rebecca gave a sigh of contentment. "I keep thanking you, Grant, and I'll say it again. That was exactly how I've imagined sex could be."

Grant stilled the hand that had been lightly caressing her back. "Is that all this was to you? That was more than just sex to me," he said, his voice gruff.

Lifting her head, she peered at him through the hair that had fallen over her eyes. "Grant…it was great. We should let it go at that." She rolled to the middle of the bed, where she sat up and reached for the sheet.

"Dammit, Rebecca, after everything we just did, why are you hiding from me?" In his frustration, Grant yanked the sheet out of her hands. Immediately Rebecca cried out, and scrambled up the mattress until she was stopped by the wall.

"Jeez! I'm not going to hit you!" he shouted. "What's going on? All I want is to take care of you— give you the things you need. I can't believe you think I'd hurt you."

Swinging his legs off the bed, he grabbed his clothes from the floor and stalked into the adjoining bath. Even standing under an icy stream of water, he couldn't drown his disappointment. But as the shower cleared his head, he tried to figure out what had gone wrong. He'd thought they'd been pretty terrific together. Okay, so maybe he'd hoped for more. Rebecca had been on his mind since the day she blew up at him in the café. He'd shared things about his marriage with her, things that not even his kids knew.

Grant honestly had thought they were making

love, not just having sex for relief. Apparently Rebecca didn't agree.

He leaned on the sink, grimacing at his reflection in the mirror, and jumped when Rebecca rapped on the closed door.

"Grant? I need to go. It's later than I thought."

He yanked opened the door, and again saw her draw back in fear. Her terror showed in her eyes and in the way she nervously rubbed her thumbs along the sleeve of her dress.

"Stop looking at me like that, Rebecca. I'm not mad and I'm not going to hurt you. It sickens me that you think I could." He rammed his arms into the sleeves of his dress shirt.

"It's not you, Grant. It's me," she said in a small voice. "That's not true. It's not me, either. It's…Jack."

"What about Jack?" Grant did up the last button on his shirt, then paused as he realized the horrible truth. "Oh, crap. He hurt you, didn't he? Rebecca, I'm so sorry. I've been a jerk. I want to know…everything. Tell me."

He led her back to the bedroom and she sank down on a corner of the mattress. "After we moved to Portland, he spent a lot of time in bars. I'm not sure if he was an alcoholic, but it was enough to make him oversleep. He was fired more than once for missing work."

Grant sat, too, but didn't crowd her.

"I'd never tasted alcohol until one night a couple

of years into our marriage. I'd gotten a raise at the insurance company, and rushed home to tell Jack. I caught him at the door saying goodbye to our new neighbor, Sonja. Oddly we didn't argue over her. I wanted to quit my night job. Jack wanted me to keep it. He stormed out, came back an hour or so later with a bouquet of flowers and two jugs of wine. No one had ever given me flowers before."

Rebecca sighed. "I was so naive. He'd been drinking enough to apologize profusely. I'm still not sure how he talked me into trying a glass of wine. Then two, then three, until I lost track of everything…including birth control. I went to work with a hangover. In Jack's favor, he felt so bad, he took a job pumping gas to make it up to me. I remember thinking it might actually be a turning point in our lives."

"Obviously not," Grant said when she fell silent.

"Well, no, idyllic moments never last. Six weeks later, I began throwing up. Sure enough, I was pregnant and I developed every side effect imaginable. My feet and legs swelled, and my doctor said I had to stop waiting tables. I told Jack he needed to find a second job. That's when he broke it to me that he'd been fired from the service station."

Grant shook his head. "You must have been worried sick."

"Try mad. But I'd seen a job posting for newspaper delivery guys. I should've known the early-morning hours would be too much for Jack. The day

I went into labor, he lost that job. It was pure luck I'd saved enough to prepay my OB and the hospital."

"So…that was Lisa?" Grant prompted, trying to break another silence.

"Lisa Louise," she mumbled, getting up and walking out to the balcony again. "Jack named her," she said, staring up at the stars. "He offered to care for Lisa, providing I went back to both jobs. It made sense because I enjoyed my work, and he hadn't found anything he wanted to do."

"Wasn't it hard to trust him at that point?"

"I still believed in him, Grant. He promised to look for work. Said later he was going on interviews, which was why he started leaving Lisa at a drop-in day care. Well, we couldn't afford any of the licensed centers, so the day care was overcrowded and understaffed. Lisa suffered from a horrid diaper rash. She cried for days. Jack yelled not to blame him, but I did. I pored over our budget and found areas to cut back so we could pay for a better center. That was six months before a gossipy neighbor told me Jack was fooling around with a woman who lived downstairs."

Grant took Rebecca's hand and she let him.

"Only a couple of people know what happened after that. Darcy knows some of it. Reliving it makes me feel stupid for letting Jack con me so often."

Squeezing her hand, Grant murmured, "Never that, Becca."

"No? He convinced me the woman was lying.

Then a water pipe broke in the insurance building and the employees were sent home. I caught Jack in our bed with the very woman he swore he wasn't sleeping with. Lisa, of course, was at day care. I told Jack I wanted a divorce, and that I was taking Lisa. I did. We moved in with a fellow waitress."

"Good for you. Wait…after all that, surely you didn't go back to him? Or did you? Is he Jordan's father, too?"

"Yes. Jack refused to sign the divorce papers. He began hounding me at the office so often it was disruptive to the other employees. Eventually, they had to let me go. I understood, but I'd signed up for a night college course. The company agreed to pay for it as part of the severance package, so I went. I don't know how Jack found out. He stalked me. One night he grabbed me and slapped me around. Another student came out of the building and Jack took off. The next day he followed me to Lisa's new day care. That night someone heaved a rock through the window of the restaurant. My room-mate said I should file for a restraining order, but honestly I was too afraid."

"Couldn't the cops arrest him for any of this?"

"There were no witnesses. Cops picked him up for questioning after he threatened the lawyer who prepared our divorce papers, but they couldn't make anything stick. I had no money to hire a second attorney. My boss at the restaurant called a friend, a fellow restaurateur, and he hired me. Jack wouldn't know where I was working. I thought it would end there."

"Don't leave me hanging, Becca. I'm sure there's worse to come."

She looked sad. "I may as well tell you the rest. Somehow Jack found me and accosted me on the way home from my night shift. It was my twenty-fifth birthday, and I was already feeling low. Not that it matters, except I'd let my guard down. Jack was worse than I'd ever seen him. Wild-eyed." Rebecca shivered and raked a hand through her hair. Grant rubbed her cold arms.

"Jack grabbed my braid and dragged me into the backseat of a car," she said woodenly. "One he'd stolen. He tore my skirt almost off, and he…raped me."

"That's enough. You don't have to say any more, Becca. It's over. Portland is miles away from San Antonio."

Nodding, Rebecca curled into the shelter of his arms. "I moved to Texas because a police officer and rape advocate, Sue Crenshaw, knew a victim-relief counselor here. She helped me file assault charges. The problem was, I'd never divorced Jack. The lawyer said a judge might do nothing more than order us into marriage counseling. This was before the marital rape laws were changed. Back then a husband had rights."

"God, Becca, please don't tear yourself apart telling me this."

"I'm almost finished. As you can imagine, my life got more complicated when I found out I was pregnant again. Thanks to Sue's connections, I managed to get a divorce, and a place at a safe house here."

"You got yourself and your daughter out of a dangerous situation. That took guts."

"It was hard at first, not knowing anyone, but little by little I got better. I took control of my life."

Grant rubbed his chin on the top of her head. "I wouldn't blame you if you never wanted to see another man. I'm so sorry. I wish I'd known before, well, before I acted like an ass."

"Which is exactly why I had to tell you, Grant. Tonight was so special. And you are the opposite of Jack. You deserved an explanation. Now, I really have to go." Slipping out of his embrace, Rebecca collected her wrap and her purse. "I wanted you to see why we can't keep seeing each other."

"Why? We have everything we need to start fresh. What you've told me is all the more reason for me to want to make your life easier. You need a new car, and you deserve some luxury—diamonds, even."

"You know, Grant, I don't recall saying I wanted anything from you. Not a car. Not a night in a five-star hotel. And certainly not diamonds. Somehow I thought you'd understand what my independence means to me. Although why I thought that, I'm not sure. You bought your seventeen-year-old son an overpriced convertible, and yourself a sports car you don't need. Not to mention you're willing to buy an eleven-year-old a three-hundred-dollar skirt. As if the problem with our older kids isn't stressful enough, you toss money around like there's no tomorrow." Her shoulders sagged as if she was giving up the fight. "I'm sorry. It's your money."

Grant had already opened the hotel room door, but now he shut it again. "Are we arguing about money? You're right, I don't understand. But if I get down on my knees and apologize for saying I want to buy you the world, can we at least go back to where we were before? I don't want this to be the end."

Rebecca met his steady gaze. "Can't you see how different we are?"

"I know we cleared the air. I also know I want to see you again. I think if you're honest with yourself, you'll agree you want to see me, too."

She took so long to answer, Grant was afraid she'd turn him down.

"Yes. I do."

Her reply was quiet, but Grant smiled wide in relief. He reached for her hand. "Okay. I'll walk you to your car. On the way we'll talk about where we go from here."

CHAPTER SEVEN

GRANT HELD the door for Rebecca and they walked side by side to the elevator. He punched the button several times. "I can't wait to go forward, Rebecca."

"We went pretty far already, if you ask me." Her eyes shone with mischief.

"Oops, hold on a second. The orchids on the table are for you. Wait here. I'll go get them."

"I can't take the flowers, Grant."

"Why not? They're hardly as extravagant as a car or diamonds."

"No, but my kids would wonder. I'm not in the habit of buying myself orchids. In fact, I can't remember the last time we had flowers in the house."

Grant shoved his hands deep into his pants pockets. "Maybe we should stop sneaking around, Rebecca. Our kids will just have to deal with it."

"I'll be honest, Grant. I'm torn. You love your kids. I love mine. We wouldn't have met except for the relationship between your son and my daughter. That situation hasn't changed. I know you don't see it as a problem, but I do."

The elevator came and they stepped inside. "I just don't think it's a big deal. Ryan says they're more like buddies."

"So what? Lisa still can't afford to go to that dance and she still needs to focus on school. I'm not going to back off just because you don't want Ryan to get mad at you."

"What does that have to do with us dating? I'm all for telling them. You're the one who wants to keep quiet because you're afraid your kids won't approve of your seeing someone. Any man. Isn't that right?"

The elevator reached the lobby and the door slid open. Rebecca marched straight out past the doorman, leaving Grant to follow or not.

"Hold up." Dashing out the door behind her, Grant grabbed her elbow to slow her down. "Running away doesn't solve anything. I'll admit that we both have to be careful dealing with our oldest kids. But I don't think keeping secrets from them is the answer. I say we bring them into the loop."

Rebecca stopped short of her car to glare at him. "Are you nuts? They'd be furious and it would only make things worse. As well, I told you Lisa's said more than once lately that she's sure her father would be the better parent. You admitted Ryan has his mother on a pedestal and you can't compete with that. How on earth would hurting them more change any of this?"

"I've been doing better with Ryan these last couple of weeks. Have you listened to Lisa's side?"

"Her reasons don't matter. She has respon- sibilities that she's ignoring. Once she starts con- tributing to her college fund again and fully brings up her grades, I'll consider reevaluation." Rebecca stalked back to where Grant had stopped. "Don't you dare lecture me, Grant. Not until you've got some kind of relationship with your own kids."

"I talked to Ryan about the dance and his inten- tions toward Lisa."

"So you say."

"I'll swear on a stack of Bibles."

"All right. How did it go? Was it civil?"

"It wasn't too bad. In fact it may have been one of our more enlightening conversations." Grant's lips twitched. "Ryan wasn't completely awake, so I think I caught him with his guard down."

"You'd really make my day if you just said you'd convinced Ryan not to attend the Spring Fling."

"The kids are going to the dance." Grant draped an arm over Rebecca's shoulders. "Have you ever heard the phrase if you can't beat 'em, join 'em?"

"You're thinking we should chaperone the dance?"

"I didn't mean that, but it's not a bad idea. I meant we should plan some kind of outing and include all four kids. If they see us behaving normally, perhaps they'll realize they aren't getting to us the way they thought and just give up."

"You think they teamed up because we—I— objected so strongly?"

"Anything is possible, Becca. What do you say? Are you game? I swear Ryan said they both want to go to college." Grant hesitated. "Uh, he also said that maybe you push Lisa too hard."

"You have no right to say that to me. You can afford to send Ryan to college no matter what kind of marks he has. Lisa needs a scholarship. Top schools look at SATs, honors classes and grades. Oh, this is hopeless. I don't know why I keep expecting you to understand."

"Nothing is hopeless." He took the key she'd pulled out of her purse and opened her car door. "Some things take more effort, is all. You and I have more going for us than not. I wish you'd give my idea a shot. We present a united front and I think they'll see it's useless to try to rebel."

"Maybe," she said after a moment of contemplation. "I don't know if it'll change Lisa's attitude but I'll try. What I do know is that I'd rather not fight with you, Grant."

"I don't want to fight with you, either, sweetheart."

"Do you have any specific ideas?"

"Actually, yes. Can you free up next Sunday afternoon? I thought we could have a barbecue at my house—without warning any of the kids. We'll be in a controlled environment where they can throw questions at us as much as they'd like. As for us, we stick together no matter what they say."

"I don't know, Grant. There are some things I don't want to get into with my kids. You know more about my life with their father than they do, and I still haven't decided how much they need to know."

"Don't you think they'll be distracted by the food and the party atmosphere? They're kids," Grant said, as Rebecca climbed into her car. He bent so they could continue to talk through the window.

"Maybe. I'm pretty sure Lisa was on next Sunday's schedule at the Tumbleweed. I saw her name listed. I think she's on for the dinner hour."

"So, a noon barbecue would be okay?"

"You're very persuasive, Grant. I'll be there, even knowing how much laundry I have piled up. Before I take off, tell me what I can bring. You've made it clear you don't cook."

"I don't want to make more work for you, Rebecca. How difficult can it be to fix hamburgers and hot dogs on a gas grill? And I know how to open chip bags. Do we need anything else?"

"Let me make a salad to round it out a bit. Do your kids prefer green or macaroni?"

"Most definitely macaroni."

Rebecca started her car. "I hope you're right about all this. I have to get going. I don't need my kids wondering why I got home so late."

"No…ah…that wouldn't be good." He frowned.

"I do want my kids to like you, Grant. Understand, though, that other than occasionally meeting Darcy, I don't go out. I expect they'll both be shocked to say the least."

"You're a tough lady to convince. I'm beginning to see why it's taken you so long to decide to date."

"You sound like Lisa and Darcy," Rebecca said. "Here's what I always tell them, Grant.... I don't date because it takes too much energy. There's always a million other things that need to come first."

"Dating when you have kids is never easy. In Germany, everyone on base knew everyone else's business. Invite a woman out for a simple drink, and the gossips had you engaged. That reminds me. Brandy announced that she wants a mom. She tried to finagle a meeting between me and her room mother, who is also a single parent. If anything, Brandy will make a bigger deal of you coming to the house than the others will."

"She's not as loyal to her real mom as Ryan?"

"She never knew Teresa, remember? There's nothing there to hold on to."

"Lisa can't remember much, if anything, about Jack, and Jordan is in the same position as Brandy. Yet they both mention him way more often than I'd like."

"Huh. It could be that my kids know their mom's never coming back. Do yours think there's a possibility you'll get back together with Jack?"

Rebecca snorted. "They ought to know better than that." She paused, as though reconsidering. "I hope they do. Although, I hear my divorced clients complain that their kids can't accept that their parents won't be reconciling. Sometimes after re-

marriage, even. My two shouldn't have any delu-
sions—we haven't even seen Jack in fifteen years,"
she said. "Enough, Grant. We could debate this all
night. I need to be on my toes tomorrow so I don't
accidentally mention your barbecue."

Grant leaned in her window and kissed her
goodbye. And he put a lot into the kiss. Everything
he still had bottled up.

"Nice," she murmured, tracing his lips with one
finger after he broke the kiss. "No greeting me like
that next Sunday. Oh, but how do we tell them we
met?"

"We have to tell them the truth. If we expect
honesty from them, Rebecca, we need to recipro-
cate. If we want them to be happy about us seeing
each other."

She hesitated, but didn't argue.

Taking her silence for agreement, Grant stepped
aside. He stood in the hotel parking lot until he saw
her taillights disappear down the street.

GRANT FOUND himself impatient for the next week
to end. His kids seemed to squabble more than
usual. Wednesday, Ryan flew out of his room
around four o'clock. "Can't you make Brandy take
that stupid clarinet someplace else?"

"She has to practice to get better, Ryan."

"Doesn't mean I should have to listen to it. I can't
believe some music teacher said she has talent."

"He said she had good embouchure, which

means how her mouth fits over the mouthpiece. That's a bit different than saying she has talent. We just need to give her a chance to learn, Ryan."

"I think I'll go see if any of the guys on the team want to grab a burger. I spent all my allowance on the tickets for the dance. Can I have an advance?"

Grant reached for his wallet, then hesitated. "I advance you a lot, Ryan. I'm going to start deducting from your next month's allowance."

"Why? It's not like you're broke, Colonel."

"I'm retired now."

"So what? You've got it all stashed somewhere. Mom told me that's why we had to leave California, because you wouldn't give her any money to keep the house there."

"That's not true, Ryan. I told your mother she didn't have to come to Germany. I took the promotion because it would mean a big difference to my pension."

"I heard Mom tell our housekeeper you'd love to sweep us under the rug like yesterday's dirt."

"Ryan, I try not to criticize your mother, but she tended to exaggerate."

"*I* don't exaggerate. You almost never called, even when I was little."

"I was in some remote sites when you were little. It's no secret that your mom and I had difficulties in our marriage and I'm sorry you've had to deal with that. I'm grateful we worked out a lot of issues after you two came to live in Germany."

"Sure, you can say that when Mom's not here to disagree."

"Dammit, Ryan!"

Father and son glared at each other until Grant hauled out his wallet and handed over a twenty-dollar bill. As he watched Ryan snatch it and stalk out, it hit him that he was guilty of exactly what Rebecca said. He let money ease his guilt, when in fact he had nothing to feel guilty about. Teresa had known how to pull his strings, and their son had picked up some of her manipulative tricks.

He closed himself in the den and reached for the phone. Rebecca was probably still at the salon, but if nothing else, he wanted to hear her voice.

"Hi," he said when she answered.

"Grant? Why are you calling? Have you changed your mind about Sunday?" Rebecca kept her voice low, as though trying not to be overheard.

"Definitely not. We're still on. Are you with a client?"

"No, I just finished and now I'm sweeping up. I have to get home soon for supper before my shift at the Tumbleweed. Is something wrong?"

"You were right about me." Briefly he relayed what had happened between him and Ryan. "I forked over twenty bucks without batting an eye. I know I didn't handle this well. What would you have done?"

"I can't tell you how to raise your children, Grant."

"I shouldn't have given him any money, should I?"

"I don't know. I don't have all the answers. It's hard to change rules late in the game. Your rules about advancing his allowance needed to be spelled out from the beginning. That's my philosophy, but the other night you told me Lisa's complained to Ryan that I'm too strict, so obviously I don't always get it right, either."

"I'm realizing that parenting is a damned difficult job no matter what the circumstances."

"You can say that again."

"Ryan's almost grown. I had airmen not much older than him in my squadron, and a lot of them were married with kids to support. I should've maybe asked Ryan to consider getting a part-time job for extra spending money."

"There you go. You found your own solution."

"A little late, but I'll be ready for him next time. Anyway, I don't want to make you late getting home. The fact is, Sunday is too far away. All day yesterday I thought about showing up at your salon with lunch."

"How do you fill your days, Grant? Not long ago Jordan reminded me that soon he and Lisa will be out of the house and I'll be on my own. I realized how much time I spend doing things for my kids. I panicked imagining what I would do with myself."

"I rattle around more than I anticipated. I have a contract to write an air force technical manual, and I'm toying with writing a history of the fighter plane I flew that's about to be replaced. The general told me he had a list of things he'd put off doing until he retired. Stuff like learning to golf, catching up on reading, going to a movie in the middle of the afternoon. I thought at the time they sounded trite. Maybe not. I am reading more. I don't think I'd like to golf alone, and movies are much more fun if you have someone to talk to afterward. I might like woodworking, or doing volunteer work at the military hospital."

"I guess you need to get serious about your projects, then."

"Or maybe someone to do these things with. Are you interested?"

"I'll use one of my son's favorite expressions. Don't hold your breath, Grant. With two kids headed for college, I don't see retirement in my future any time soon. The hours I'll have to fill are the ones I currently spend doing their laundry, grocery shopping and fixing meals for three. Really, Grant, much as I'd like to chat, I have to run or get caught in the five-thirty traffic."

"Sure. I need to go check on Brandy, anyway. I can't hear her clarinet. Sometimes silence isn't so bad."

They laughed and said goodbye.

He was in a much better mood by the time he hung up.

GRANT AND BRANDY were eating grilled cheese sandwiches in the kitchen when Ryan blew in from his evening out.

"I bought ice cream," he said, popping two containers in the freezer.

"Did you get rocky road?" Brandy asked.

"Of course. And chocolate-chocolate chip."

"My teacher says eating too much chocolate will give you zits," Brandy announced.

"I have a cream for that. A dermatologist at the base clinic in Germany gave me a prescription," Ryan said. He ran a hand over his face, and Grant noticed his son needed a shave.

When had that happened?

"I don't recall you visiting a dermatologist, Ryan."

"Big surprise there. You were never around, Colonel."

"I stopped being a colonel when I left the air force. I'm just Dad now."

"Yeah, Ryan." Brandy jumped up from her chair and looped her arms around her father's neck. "I like having Daddy home all the time."

"Right! You're sucking up so he'll get you a puppy."

The kids started a litany of "am nots" and "are toos" until Grant put his fingers to his lips and whistled loudly.

"Now that I have your attention, I have something to tell you both." Grant waited for both kids to look at him. "I was talking to a friend the other day. I invited their family over for a casual barbecue on Sunday. Around twelve-hundred hours. Plan on being up and looking presentable."

Ryan scoffed and nearly tipped over a chair in his haste to leave the room. "I'm not under your command, Colonel. You can't order me to help entertain your old air force buds."

"This isn't a military family, Ryan."

"I don't give a rat's behind who they are. I'll stay in my room. Or maybe I'll ask some of the guys if they want to go to a movie downtown."

"Does your friend have kids my age?" Brandy asked.

"No, honey. The kids are older. Nearer Ryan's age. And, son," Grant added with steel in his voice, "staying in your room or going out isn't an option. You see your friends every day at school. Sunday is going to be family time."

"You can't force me to stick around and be bored stiff."

"Fine. But I expect you to at least meet them. Then you can leave if you like."

"That's stupid. Maybe I'll say goodbye on my way out. By the way, I was wrong on the date of our school dance. It's this coming Saturday night. I'll be home late. Don't bother waiting up."

"You'll be home at twelve on the dot," Grant said. "Or I take the keys to the convertible. And see that you drive carefully, especially if you have friends riding in your car."

"Like you care," Ryan muttered, still lingering in the doorway.

"I do, regardless of what you think." Grant

wanted to say more, but instead set a hand on Brandy's shoulder. "Tomorrow after school, would you like to go look at puppies?"

"Yes!" Brandy shouted.

"We're just looking, mind you. No promises."

"Yes!" she said again. "Thank you, thank you, thank you, Daddy!"

Ryan rolled his eyes. "Brandy, remember what I said. This proves I'm right."

Tears suddenly filled Brandy's eyes. Ryan headed for his room and slammed his door so hard Grant felt the kitchen table vibrate. Brandy only cried harder.

"Brandy, what did he mean? Why are you bawling?"

"I want a puppy, but Ryan said I shouldn't let you get me one, 'cause you're only trying to buy our affections." She threw herself so hard against Grant, she almost knocked him out of his chair. "Ryan says that means you don't really love us."

Grant held his sobbing daughter tightly. "Your brother has no right to say such horrible things to you."

Brandy sniffled. "So, you do love us?"

"More than anything. Honey, I'm sorry there was ever any doubt."

"Did you love Mama?"

Grant's heart sank. Why, why had this come up now, days before he wanted his kids to meet Rebecca?

"Brandy, I wish you kids hadn't lost your mother.

She loved Ryan very much, and would've loved you equally. She and I had our problems, but we both loved you before you were born. If Ryan claims I let my career get in the way, he's right. I'm here now, though, and I'm trying to be a better dad. One thing I'm not doing is trying to buy your love with a puppy or anything else, as Ryan suggested. I'll make it clear to him, too, that love is given, not bought."

"Oh, so I can't have a puppy?" Brandy's face crumpled.

"If you want to *look* at puppies tomorrow, we will. But I'm not promising to bring one home. Understood?"

"I'm paying 'cause you're mad at Ryan. That's not fair, Daddy. He said he asked for a car and you felt guilty about not loving us, so you bought him the Mustang. And you gave him money for Lisa's flowers last week."

Grant swore, then bit his tongue when Brandy's eyes widened. "I guarantee, Ryan and I will be having words about all this." Later. He didn't want to open this can of worms before Rebecca's visit on Sunday.

"Don't yell at him, Daddy. I just want us to get along. Ryan never got along with Nanny Ada. They hollered at each other all the time. I was scared she'd leave. She said she would if we weren't good."

"Brandy, that's news to me, too. Ada sent me reports each week and never said a word about fighting with Ryan. I'm sorry. I would've replaced her if I'd known."

"Well, Nanny Lurette was worse. She spanked me for saying I didn't want her to be my mama. But I didn't. She smelled like smoke. I heard Ryan tell his friend Joe that Nanny Lurette wanted to marry you and be our step-mama."

Grant had known Lurette had hoped to marry him. He'd never so much as dated her, but he supposed the security he could offer had been the main attraction. He hadn't realized his kids knew, but he realized that had been naive. "Brandy, we have a number of issues to clear up. I swear I never considered marrying Lurette, and I should've been more careful about your other nannies. I relied on an agency and neighbors to give me feedback. It seems I should've checked with you and Ryan. I'm sorry I didn't."

"Ryan says all stepmothers are wicked like Cinderella's. Is that true? If it is, I don't want one. I know I said I want you to meet my room mom. Can I take that back? I don't know if Mrs. Sanchez would be wicked, but maybe she would."

"Brandy, stop! Before I marry anyone, I'd ask for your opinion and Ryan's."

"And then what?"

"And then I'd listen to what you said. Let's talk about something else. Do you want ice cream for dessert, or not?"

"Yes. I feel better now, Daddy. I hope Ryan will, too, after you talk to him. He thinks you'll do whatever you want, no matter what we say."

As Grant and Brandy dug into the rocky road, he worried that maybe he shouldn't have invited Rebecca and her family over. At least not until he solved some of the issues with Ryan.

But he wanted to date Rebecca openly. Besides, this was his life, and as much as he wanted his kids to be happy, there were some aspects he wouldn't let them control. The sooner Ryan and Brandy learned that, the better.

CHAPTER EIGHT

SUNDAY MORNING, Grant was rudely awakened by the screeching sounds of Brandy's clarinet.

Ryan, who'd come in well after curfew the night before, pounded on the wall between their bedrooms and yelled at her to knock it off.

Grant wished he could ignore them both. Thursday and Friday, Brandy hadn't gotten the puppy she wanted. She'd pouted and refused to eat with her dad ever since.

Grant's talk with Ryan at two-thirty that morning hadn't gone well, either. Ryan had accused his dad of waiting up to check his breath for alcohol. Their heated discussion ended with Grant taking away the keys to Ryan's Mustang.

Ryan's parting shot had been vicious. "I'll graduate soon. Then you can't boss me around. I'll move out the minute I can. Believe me, I can't wait." He ended with words not fit for Brandy's ears. That infuriated Grant more when he found her listening to their fight, and crying at her door.

Grant leaned up on one elbow and reached for his

bedside clock. It was later than he'd thought. Almost eleven hundred hours to be exact. Rebecca and her kids were due in one short hour. Grant needed to make some kind of peace with his own kids before she arrived. Plus he needed to vacuum and make patties out of the ground beef he'd thawed overnight.

Flinging off his sheet, he stuck his head into the hall. "That's enough!" he bellowed. "Ryan, rise and shine. Shower and get dressed. *Nice* shorts, okay? Brandy, put away the clarinet, and pick up your room. Our guests will be here soon, so we need to get our act together."

"I don't care about your stupid guests," Ryan shouted back. "I'm going to phone J.J. and have him pick me up for the movies early. If he can't come get me, I'll walk downtown. I'm not going to pretend I want to meet any friends of yours."

Grant shut his bedroom door with a loud bang. He stalked into the shower and turned on a blast of water as cold as he could get. Lukewarm was the coldest it ever got in San Antonio. Not so different from what he'd gotten used to in the Middle East. At least here he *had* running water.

It was 11:20 when Grant finished making his bed and taking his dirty clothes to the laundry room down the hall.

He ran into Brandy, and was so shocked at her appearance he couldn't move. Brandy had tried to braid her hair in lots of little braids. Tufts of blond hair stuck out every which way. She wore too-tight red jeans and a cropped purple tank top Grant had never seen. This was the child he'd told Rebecca wanted everything to match. As if that wasn't enough, she'd also painted her nails. Black.

"Brandy, I am trying very hard to remain calm. But where in God's name did that getup come from? No, doesn't matter," he said, closing his eyes and rubbing his temples. "Change into something that fits. Brush your hair. And…clean off that ghoulish nail polish."

"But this morning on TV one of the Cheetah Girls had an outfit that looked just like this. Except she probably had somebody braid her hair. I couldn't see the back of mine." Brandy's lower lip quivered.

"Honey, costumes worn on TV are too…uh… too…" Grant searched for a word to replace *out-landish,* the first that popped into his head. "Flam-boyant. Flashy. Please go put on regular clothes. And, honey, your hair is naturally so pretty. That's the girl I want my friend to see."

"I messed up my nails, and I don't have any polish remover. Will you drive me to the store to buy some, Daddy?"

Grant looked at his watch and mentally counted to ten. "We really don't have time to go now. Our guests are due soon. Just do your best with the clothes and your hair. Where's Ryan?"

"He went back to bed."

Grant rubbed his sternum to soothe the burn spreading through his chest. There was still so much to do. He needed to calm down. How had Teresa made entertaining look so easy? There must be a trick to having everything ready together.

He knocked hard on Ryan's door and yelled, "Get up this instant!" Grant heard the doorbell at the same time as he stuck his head in Ryan's room. "They're here. You have two minutes to get your butt in the shower, then out to say a civil hello, or I guarantee you won't drive the Mustang until you're thirty." He used his best military commander's voice, and it resonated. Ryan threw off his covers.

Brandy rushed out of her room looking far better than she had earlier. Suddenly shy, she hid behind Grant when he answered the door.

It did his heart good to see Rebecca's son acting bored and her daughter pouting. Her kids looked as if they'd rather be at the dentist's.

Rebecca broke off from whatever she'd been saying and smiled. Grant figured she didn't want to be caught scolding her kids for surliness. She stepped in front of them, her arms clasping a large glass salad bowl.

"Rebecca, I'm so glad you found us," Grant greeted her. "Let me take that dish. It looks heavy. This is my daughter, Brandy. Honey, say hello to my friend Mrs. Geroux. Uh, Rebecca." He stumbled over his words in the face of unquestionably hostile teens.

Rebecca maintained her grip on the salad bowl.

"Hi," Brandy said, peering out from around her

dad. Seeing Rebecca's daughter, she whispered loudly, "Daddy, isn't that girl Ryan's friend? The one we saw hugging him at his ball game?"

Jordan Geroux suddenly straightened. "Your voice is familiar. You called one night, asking for Mom. What's going on, Mom?"

Lisa hissed, "Mom, this so sucks! That *is* Ryan's dad." She eyed Grant, then whirled on Brandy. "You both came to Ryan's game. He didn't want you there. *Mother,* are you trying to wreck my life?"

Rebecca shrugged feebly, imploring Grant to help get them out of this mess.

He was desperately trying to think when his son shuffled into the hall. The first person Ryan saw was Lisa. The boy hadn't bothered making himself presentable. Embarrassed, he tried smoothing both hands over his hair. "What the hell, Colonel? These are your friends?" Rushing over to stand beside Lisa, Ryan said, "Why not just admit you've never met Lisa's mother before?" Ryan said, his voice rough and challenging. "You did this to embarrass me in front of Lisa."

"Ryan Arthur Lane, I have had it with your attitude." Grant held up a hand to quiet his son. "Not only do I know Rebecca, we've been dating for weeks."

The silence that followed was so profound, the twelve cheery *cuckoos* heralding the hour would've been comical if not for the tense atmosphere.

Rebecca lost her grip on the bowl as all four kids

stared at her. It struck the tile floor, spewing macaroni salad and broken glass across the entryway.

Grant froze. Then as if choreographed, those same mutinous gazes turned on him, demanding he retract his preposterous statement.

Only he couldn't. With an outward calm that belied the storm raging inside him, Grant touched Rebecca's pale face. "We promised to tell the truth, didn't we, Becca?" He looked from her to the kids, then back to her again. "God, Rebecca, are you hurt?" Only when she shook her head did he ask, "Was anyone cut by flying glass?" But the kids were too shocked to answer. "Rebecca, I'm so sorry. After all the work you put into making that salad..." His words trailed off as he lifted Brandy away from the glass shards. Bending, he checked the little girl's bare feet and legs for cuts.

Rebecca set her purse on a wooden entry table, then knelt to pick up the pieces.

Glaring at the older teens, who remained unmoving, Grant slid a hand under Rebecca's arm and gently drew her to her feet. "I'll clean up. You and the kids go on out to the patio. There's a cooler with a selection of sodas."

"Not on your life," she muttered. "You're not leaving me alone with them now. What were you thinking? How does this solve any of our problems?"

Grant's normally clear eyes were stormy. "I've had a...challenging morning. Anyway, it would've come out sooner or later."

"Rather it be later," Rebecca admitted with a sigh.

Brandy, at least, smiled at Rebecca. "So, are you gonna, like, be our new mother?" she asked breathlessly.

Then it was as if the stunned teens came back to life. Ryan yanked his sister back. "Don't be an idiot. We have a mother."

"We do not!" Brandy shouted. "She's dead!"

The girl batted her brother's hand away, as Lisa said hotly, "And *we* have a dad. How long have you been cheating on Daddy?" She pointed dramatically at Grant. "Is *he* the reason you don't want me seeing Ryan? This is so sick. How could you do this to me, Mother?"

The only kid not chiming in was Jordan. He seemed dazed by the revelations.

"Stop!" Grant's low voice demanded silence. "Brandy, get me a broom and dustpan from the kitchen. I'll clean up, then we'll sit on the patio like civilized people, and each of you will have a turn to vent."

"I'm not listening to anything my mother has to say." Lisa shot Rebecca a dirty look, and grabbed Ryan's arm. "Will you take me someplace else? To Darcy's. I'll move in with her."

"Good grief!" Rebecca started forward, but was stopped by the sound of crunching glass under her feet.

"Sorry, I can't drive you," Ryan said with a sneer. "The colonel took my car keys last night because I missed my frigging curfew."

Brandy ran back into the hall carrying the broom and dustpan for her dad.

"Tell the truth, Ryan." Grant swept up the sticky macaroni with short, angry strokes. "I took your keys because you mouthed off to me and upset Brandy."

The boy rolled his eyes and looked away.

"Then I'll walk to Darcy's," Lisa declared, her pretty face pinched. "Jordan, are you coming with me?"

"Why?" Jordan seemed confused.

"Because I bet *she* has deliberately hidden us from Dad. For all we know, Ryan's dad could be why our parents split." In her anger, Lisa whirled on Grant. "Is Mom why you moved to San Antonio? Ryan said it was odd, since none of you knew a soul here. Never mind, you'll both just lie to us. I'll find out the truth from my own father."

Jordan rallied. "Like that makes any sense, Lisa. You're being stupid."

Rebecca spoke up with enough force to stop her daughter's stomp to the front door. In a voice rigid with tension, she said, "I planned that one day soon we three would sit down and talk about your dad. I *hadn't* planned to have an audience." She hesitated, took a deep breath and darted an apologetic glance toward Grant. "Jack Geroux is in jail. Why he's there is irrelevant. He's out of our lives nevertheless."

This time not even the cuckoo clock brought any relief to the absolute silence in the room.

"I don't believe you!" Lisa shouted, scrubbing

away her tears. She yanked open the door and ran down the walkway.

Visibly distressed, Rebecca tried to follow. Grant dropped the broom and stayed her with a hand. "She's so upset with you, Becca, nothing you say now will get through to her. Maybe you should send Ryan." He drew his keys out of his pocket and tossed them to his son.

Rebecca studied the handsome boy, very like his father. He appeared subdued, but also worried about Lisa. She nodded without speaking.

Grant said, "Okay, son, make sure she doesn't do anything foolish."

"You shouldn't have dumped all this on her at once." Ryan glared at both adults.

"You're probably right," Grant said, walking his son to the door. "You mentioned going to a movie with friends. Do you have enough money to include Lisa? She's had a shock, but she needs to understand her mom's not the bad guy here. You know imprisonment is serious business, Ryan."

Ryan jingled the keys. "This is real decent of you." Turning back to Rebecca, the boy said, "Mrs. Geroux, what should I do if Lisa doesn't want to go home after the movie? Assuming she even agrees to come."

Rebecca rubbed her hands up and down her pant legs. "I guess let her go to Darcy's. Please, just go after her. I'd never forgive myself if something happens to her when she's this upset."

Ryan left. Jordan sidled to the door and gazed

down the street. "Lisa was sitting on the curb, Mom. She got in the car with Ryan," he announced. He shut the door, but it was plain he wanted to ask something else.

"Jordan, have Brandy show you where to find the soft drinks," Grant urged. "Your mom and I will be out as soon as we have this mess cleaned up."

"Oh, you put pickles and mustard in your macaroni salad," Brandy exclaimed, staring at the mound in the dustpan. "That's my favorite. Before you leave, will you write down how to make it, Mrs. Geroux?"

"Certainly, Brandy. But I'm not sure if Jordan and I should stay now. I'll get you the recipe, though."

Grant picked up the dustpan. "Don't go. We have loads of food. What can you do from home, anyway?"

"True. Is that okay with you, Jordan?"

"I *am* hungry, so we might as well."

"I'll show you where the sodas are," Brandy said excitedly, the earlier drama apparently forgotten.

"Tell you what, Brandy, along with writing down my salad recipe, I'll give you the name of a really good beginner's cookbook. Better yet, you can have our copy. Jordan and Lisa have graduated to more involved recipes."

"I like to cook," Jordan said, hunching a bit as he followed the younger girl to the back door. "It's cleaning up the kitchen afterward that I don't like."

"No one likes that," his mother called after him.

Grant accompanied the kids to the kitchen, where

he emptied the full dustpan. He returned carrying a plastic container filled with cleaning supplies.

"I'm sorry you had to see me and Lisa like that," Rebecca said, making sure the kids closed the patio door. "Someday I'll need to tell her and Jordan why Jack's in jail, but not today. From what Sue Crenshaw told me about the trial, Jack apparently got into a drunken argument outside his apartment building with a woman who lived downstairs. An eyewitness said the woman swung at Jack with her purse. He hit her, and she lost her balance and fell backward off the stoop. She hit her head on the sidewalk and died. A jury called it involuntary manslaughter. With Jack's history of violence, the judge sentenced him to the maximum of fifteen years. Every time he comes up for parole Sue says some infraction keeps him in. I just shouldn't have blurted it all out to the kids like I did, Grant."

"It was my fault. I started it by telling them we were dating. I'm sorry, too." Grant's forehead creased as he frowned.

"I'm relieved it came out, Grant. Now I can start dealing with the fallout instead of avoiding it."

Looking doubtful, Grant dragged an upright vacuum from the hall closet, plugged it in and turned it on. He rolled it across the tiles to suck up any missed glass.

After Grant put the vacuum away, Rebecca knelt and scrubbed the greasy spot. "Lisa has every right to be angry. But what really hurt me was when she accused me of lying about Jack. All I've ever wanted was to protect her and Jordan." She stood and capped the cleaner. "Whenever I imagined telling them about Jack, I never expected them to take his side."

"You should've told me the whole story the other day."

"I know. Jack frightens me, but I haven't wanted the kids to be afraid."

"They may not be. Kids don't operate by our rules. We're a pair, aren't we? Trying to shield our kids, and ending up hurting them. I haven't told Ryan his mother suffered an anxiety disorder. I guess I've been afraid he'd think that I was trying to blame Teresa for things he's mad at me for. She was fine when she took her meds. I don't know why she sometimes didn't."

Rebecca watched Grant repack the cleaning supplies. "I think we still have a long way to go when it comes to being honest with our kids."

"We built a framework today."

"You think now it'll be easier to sit and have heart-to-hearts?"

"I do. Come wash up in the kitchen. Then we'll see what Jordan and Brandy are up to."

When Grant and Rebecca got outside they found Brandy and Jordan drinking sodas, but seeming distant and uneasy with each other.

Grant tried to break the ice. "The weather's so

great, do you want to swim before or after we eat?"
he asked. "Our pool is heated, Jordan."

"I didn't bring trunks or a towel," the boy said.
"Mom didn't tell us where we were going." He
scowled in Rebecca's direction.

"The casita has plenty of extra towels, and I think
Ryan has an extra suit in there that should fit."

"What's a casita?" Jordan asked, peering around.

"That's what our Realtor called it. It's like a
guest house."

"Wow, you have a guest house as well as this big
home?" Rebecca looked over to where Brandy was
pointing at a bungalow set back from the far end of
the pool. She thought that was excessive, but kept
her thoughts to herself.

"The casita was just a bonus. I hoped my folks
would stay there when they visit," Grant said. "Not
that they will—they hate flying. Funny, since that's
all I like to do. I offered to pay their airfare if they'd
come to Germany and take care of Brandy after she
was born, but they couldn't face the flight. So, they
rarely see their grandchildren."

Jordan glanced sympathetically at Brandy. "I
thought Lisa and I were the only kids who didn't
know their grandparents."

Rebecca chose a soda from the cooler. "Your
grandparents would never approve of your logo
shirts, TV, video games and iPod. They're super religious," she explained to Brandy. "They believe in
a simpler life."

"Daddy's mom and dad send Ryan and me birthday and Christmas cards with money. That's cool."

"We could visit them on one of your school breaks. I've just gotten used to sporadic contact. But if it's important to you, we'll go. I know it's hard to believe, Brandy, but I'm doing my best to learn about this parenting stuff."

"It's never easy, Grant," Rebecca said. "Until today, I actually thought I was doing a good job raising my kids. I guess some days are better than others."

"You're pretty," Brandy said unexpectedly. "And you cook for your kids."

Grant laughed, grabbed his daughter and pretended he was going to toss her into the pool, clothes and all. "Hey, I'm cooking for you now, as soon as you tell me what you want to eat." Grant deposited his giggling child back on her chair.

"I'll take a hamburger," Jordan said. "Maybe a hot dog, too, since we won't have any macaroni salad."

"You've got it," Grant said. "I do have lettuce, tomatoes, pickles and chips."

"Are the tomatoes and pickles sliced?" Rebecca asked. "If not, I'll go do that. Jordan, why don't you go for a swim? I notice you haven't taken your eyes off the pool," she teased.

"I'll show you the cabinet where Ryan keeps his extra suits," Brandy volunteered, popping out of her seat. "Mine is in my room, so I'll change there. And we have this really cool basketball hoop that floats on the water. It's hard to hit, but fun to try. Do you wanna play?"

"Sure." Jordan shrugged.

Once the kids were changed, Rebecca and Grant returned to the kitchen to prepare the food. Grant paused to gaze out the window. Brandy and Jordan were shouting and laughing in the pool. "Those two seem to be getting along famously. It's a shame our older kids left." He moved in behind Rebecca, and ran kisses up the back of her neck. "I like having you here like this." His voice was rough with emotion. "I hope Lisa's outburst won't keep you from seeing me, Becca."

"I'm so worried about her. Today is the second time she's mentioned hooking up with her dad. Oh, I know she has no idea where he is…but she's so angry."

"I'm sure she'll calm down. Kids fly off, but get over being mad fast."

"I hope so. This is nice. Under other circumstances it could be relaxing. Like I told you, it's been a long time since we've done anything fun together."

Grant turned her around and gave her a more satisfying kiss. "Why don't we designate Sunday as family fun day? The kids and I haven't visited the Alamo, or the Presidio. Or we could take a boat out on the river. We can talk about what we want to do over lunch."

"Whoa, not so fast," Rebecca cautioned. "I realize money isn't a huge object for you, Grant, but I'm still paying for repairs to my car, and I have to replace my garbage disposal. I really don't have extra for anything else."

"Believe it or not, I can appreciate that. Will you consider letting me cover the costs? I'd like us all to spend time together."

"I don't want to be in your debt, Grant. Plus, I worry that our relationship is just creating more problems with Lisa and Ryan. The whole point of coming here today was to present a united front. But now they're off doing heaven knows what. Do you think Lisa even went to the movies with Ryan?"

"Yes, or he would've come back." Grant frowned as he picked up the hamburger patties. "Why do you keep pulling away from me?"

Rebecca arranged the sliced tomatoes on a plate. "Because we're so different, Grant."

Rebecca could see Grant's unhappiness in the stubborn set of his lips.

"What are we doing? Either we're trying to make our families mesh, or we need to say the hell with it," he said.

"If it were just me, I'd quit my part-time job and be with you every spare minute. My life is more complicated than that. So is yours."

"Maybe." He'd turned to watch their kids again. They'd tired of playing water basketball, and climbed out of the pool. "Brandy's not a problem, but I have a lot of work to do with Ryan. It's not easy since I waited so long. But I'm not willing to give up on him—or on us, Rebecca. Will you at least let me run some Sunday get-together ideas by Jordan and Brandy?"

"All right. If you keep the costs down. You all can come to my house and I'll cook. We don't always have to come here just because you have the bigger house."

"Fine by me. Hey, didn't you say Ryan offered to install a new disposal for you? That's a good project for one Sunday. Or a weeknight even. Jordan and I can help, too."

"I suppose. I'll let you know when I can afford to pick up a new unit. Would you mind showing Jordan how to use the tools? He's sadly lacked having a man in his life."

The back door opened and the kids came in.

"We're starving," Brandy announced. "What's taking you so long?"

Grant tweaked Brandy's nose. "Well, as usual, your dad hadn't done any prep. But thanks to Rebecca, we're just about ready now. Are you kids going to change clothes before we eat?"

"I am," both exclaimed. Jordan's voice was muffled from the towel he'd flung over his head. "It's clouding over. We'd better hurry and eat or it may even hail on us." He draped the towel around his neck.

"If it does," Rebecca said, "wait ten minutes and the sun will come out again. That's how it is in Texas, especially in the spring. Go change. Grant will have a burger and a dog waiting."

The kids squealed and took off in opposite directions. Grant carried the plate of meat to a built-in grill on the patio. He turned a knob and blue flames shot up, then died back.

"That's a fancy grill," Rebecca said, following behind him. "Mine uses messy charcoal."

"A builder owned this house before me. We're lucky he put in extra amenities."

"I'm lucky I qualified for the house we have. Lisa and I lived in a women's shelter at first. The advocate I told you about, Sue Crenshaw, arranged it. She put me in touch with social workers here, who later helped me find a cheap apartment. They provided a visiting nurse after Jordan was born, too. It was a struggle, but I hated taking aid and food stamps. Everyone looks at you differently."

"You've done a great job of making a life for your family," Grant said. He smiled warmly as he set the burgers and hot dogs over the flame. "I wish you didn't have to work two jobs."

"Yeah, well, what doesn't kill us makes us stronger."

"Do you keep in touch with Sue?"

"We talk on the phone because I don't have e-mail. Anyway, she lets me know what's happening with Jack. She gets notified each time he comes up for parole. The last time I talked to Sue, she reminded me his sentence is up this summer. It's not likely, but I'm a little concerned he'll track me down."

"He doesn't know where you are, right?"

"Not so far as I know. I lived here a year before I applied for a driver's license, or used a bank.

Frankly, I worried a lot after I got a better job where they needed my social security number."

"I found you through the online telephone directory. It was even easier than I expected. I wish he wasn't getting out so soon. Now I'll worry, too."

"I'm not going to let him have that kind of power over me, Grant. Really, I doubt he cares enough to look me up after all these years. Shh, here comes Jordan. I'm sure he'll have more questions for me later."

"It's only natural for your kids to wonder about their dad."

Rebecca frowned at Grant, who'd turned to flip the hamburgers. "I hope my kids will realize that they don't need him. If Jack did something bad enough to be locked up, he's no one they should know."

"That's probably very true. From what I've seen, they're both smart kids."

"Who's smart?" Jordan suddenly appeared behind them, and sniffed the air. "Man, those smell great. All that water basketball made me hungry. I didn't know what you wanted me to do with the swimsuit and towel, so I rolled them together and put them on that bench." He pointed.

"That's good. I'll toss them in with the next load of laundry." Grant looked around. "Hmm. I wonder what's keeping Brandy."

"I'll go check on her." Rebecca stopped at the sliding-glass door. "Jordan, help yourself to a burger. While I'm gone, tell Grant what you think is wrong with our garbage disposal. He's offered to fix it, or replace it if we need to."

Jordan darted a surprised glance at his mom's back as she went into the house. "Lisa's so not gonna be happy about that. She brought Ryan home to fix it, but Mom practically threw him out before he had a chance. That's what ticked Lisa off. She and Mom have been bickering ever since."

"I thought I'd have Ryan and you help. Um…is that a bad idea?"

Jordan took a paper plate from the table and Grant slid a burger onto it. "If you and my mom are dating, are you thinking about getting married?" Jordan said unexpectedly.

"Jordan, you really need to talk to your mom about that. I shouldn't have even said anything."

"Did you know my dad?"

"Goodness, no. Lisa got that part completely wrong. I only met your mom a couple of months ago. I liked her right off, so I asked her out."

The door slid open and Rebecca and Brandy stepped out onto the patio. They chatted away, and Grant smiled to see them getting along. His heart beat faster when Brandy spun around, and said, "Daddy, look at my hair. Mrs. Geroux can French braid! My friend Kiley…her mom fixes her hair like this, and it's so cool. Do you like it?"

"You're beautiful, honey. Hey, grab plates or these burgers will be burned."

"Grant, is it all right if Brandy calls me Rebecca?

I know kids in Texas are told to call adults ma'am and sir, but ma'am makes me feel ancient."

"Whatever you two work out is fine," Grant said. "Jordan, call me Grant."

"Lisa said Ryan calls you Colonel."

Grant shut off the grill and joined them at the table. "Ryan grew up on base where people went by rank more than name. Now that I'm retired, I'm just Grant."

Brandy set her hot dog down. "Ryan calls you Colonel 'cause it makes you mad. Well, he said 'it pisses you off,' but I'm not supposed to say that."

Grant paused with his burger halfway to his mouth. "Brandy!"

Rebecca choked back a laugh. "It's such a relief, Grant, to hear you don't have perfect children, either."

"What do you mean, *either?*" Jordan acted miffed. "I'm perfect."

Rebecca smiled. "You don't give me much to complain about."

"Meaning Lisa does?" Jordan shot back, his mood suddenly changing. "I heard you tell Darcy that Lisa got off track after she met Ryan. Why don't you like him—if you're dating his dad?"

Rebecca paused to wipe her hands on a napkin. "You're fishing, Jordan. That's between me and your sister." She turned to Grant. "Since Jordan's finished eating, he and I should take off. Lisa's due at the Tumbleweed for the dinner hour, but she may think it will hurt me if she ditches work. If she doesn't show up, I'll have to take her shift. My boss is a nice man who doesn't deserve to be caught in our family problems."

"I hope you don't think Ryan will encourage her. I don't think he will," Grant said. "If you must leave, take a soda for the road. And let me know what's happening with Lisa. If I find out Ryan's causing Lisa to misbehave, he and I will have it out."

"He won't listen," Brandy said. "Ryan's always saying you made Mama cry, so you're the wrong person to show him how to be a man. He says that all the time, Daddy." She got up and hugged Grant. "I don't like you and Ryan fighting, 'cause I love you both. I feel bad for Ryan, but…I never knew Mama."

Rebecca touched Brandy's shoulder. "You should love your dad and brother equally. Grant, we need to stop discussing these issues in front of the kids." She smiled down at Brandy. "Honey, Lisa's never held a grudge. As for Ryan, his problems with your dad are nothing to do with you. Speak up for yourself. Tell Ryan you don't want to be put in the middle."

"Okay, I'll try. I feel better just telling Daddy. I'm glad you came over for a barbecue, Rebecca. I hope you come back when you can stay longer. You, too, Jordan. I'm not as good at water basketball as Ryan, but I had fun. He thinks I'm a pest and doesn't like to play with me."

Jordan turned red and shuffled toward the door. "You did okay for a girl."

His mother rolled her eyes. "Man! You'd better

watch that attitude if you want me to teach you how to drive next year."

Deliberately provocative, Jordan tilted his head to one side and said, "If you don't scare Grant away, Mom, maybe he'll teach me."

"I don't scare easily," Grant said.

Rebecca gave Grant's arm a warning nudge as she followed Jordan out of the house.

"I don't," he repeated, clearly unrepentant for bragging.

Rebecca refused to acknowledge his claims. "Bye, Grant. Bye, Brandy. I apologize for having to eat and run."

Their hosts waved as she and Jordan got in her car.

A soft smile spread over Rebecca's lips. It was enough out of character for her son to look over at her in confusion. "Okay, Mom, what gives with you and Mr. Lane?"

"He's a thoughtful and considerate man."

"I guess you like him a lot, huh?"

"I don't know yet. In many ways he's out of my league." Her voice trailed off.

"I know I'm just a kid," Jordan muttered, "but, do you like him more than Dad?"

Rebecca eased off the gas. "That's not a fair comparison. I loved your father when we got married, but building a life away from everything and everyone you know is stressful. There was a lot of pressure and your dad couldn't handle failure."

"Lisa thinks you're too hard on her. She said so."

"Your sister has a lot of freedom," Rebecca said huffily.

"Not when it comes to dating. And now that she knows you and Mr. Lane are dating, look out!"

"I need to talk to Lisa. Really talk. We haven't been communicating well lately."

"Because you hate Ryan. She doesn't like to sneak around."

"I don't *hate* Ryan. I don't want your sister sneaking around, either. I love her. I want what's best for both of you, Jordan."

"We know that. It bugs Lisa more than me that you never talk to us about our grandparents, or Dad. Mostly him. She used to make up stories that he was somebody important, like an FBI agent or CIA. Somebody who had to stay away or risk his life."

"You're kidding? I had no idea. That couldn't be further from the truth."

"Yeah, that's what you said today. I think that upset Lisa more than finding out you were dating Ryan's dad. Lisa sorta idolizes Dad."

"Why? She can't have actual memories of him. She was only two when I left him."

Jordan shrugged. "I dunno. I can't picture him. I don't look like him, do I?"

Rebecca swung into their carport, and turned to examine her son. "Lisa is blond like him. Your eyes are like mine and my mom's. You definitely have my red hair. But, honey, your dad wasn't bad-looking. He had a temper and that's what got him into trouble. I really suspect he was abused by his father. Jordan, I can honestly say you are nothing like any of the Geroux men. Okay, enough family history. Let's go inside. I need to phone the restaurant. I hope Lisa went to work. Otherwise I'll be worried sick."

They went in, and Rebecca headed for the kitchen phone. Jordan took off toward his bedroom, but reappeared at once. "Mom," he said, sounding shaken. "Lisa's cleaned out her room. I didn't go in, but her door is open. And her closet is empty. She stripped her bed and took our laptop. She took everything."

Rebecca tightened her hand on the receiver. "There's a message. Maybe she called." But it wasn't Lisa's voice on the machine.

"Rebecca, pick up if you're there. It's Darcy. I don't know what's happened between you and Lisa, but she showed up on my doorstep asking to stay. I'm happy to have her. My babysitter quit last night. But you need to tell me if you want me to send her home. She has that boy, Ryan, with her. He's helping her carry her stuff upstairs." The call ended abruptly. The second message was also from Darcy.

"Are you still gone? Lisa left for work, or at least Ryan said he'd drop her at the Tumbleweed. Call me ASAP. Lisa's not making much sense. She's so p.o.'d."

Rebecca hit Erase. She slumped against the wall,

muttering, "I'll have to take back what I said about your sister not holding a grudge." She snatched up the phone again. "I'd better call Grant and the Tumbleweed. What a mess."

CHAPTER NINE

"Jordan, I'm going to call Grant first to see if Ryan has come home. That way, Grant can ask him if he dropped Lisa at work, and I won't have to check up on her at the restaurant." Rebecca found Grant's number in her purse, and was reminded of their romantic interlude. Had it really only been a week ago?

She dialed, and felt an odd sense of relief. Not so long ago she'd had no one to share her concerns with. He answered and the sound of his voice further eased her panic. "Grant? It's Rebecca. Lisa's moved all her things to Darcy's. Darcy left a message saying Ryan helped Lisa move, and also took her to work. Do you know if he did?"

"He got home not five minutes after you left. Let me switch phones, and take this call in my bedroom." There was silence for a minute, until Grant picked up again. "Are you still with me, Becca?"

"I'm here. Don't keep me in suspense. Did Ryan mention Lisa?"

"Yes. We had a surprisingly civil conversation.

That in itself is progress. He handed back his keys, and politely asked if I'd allow him to take the car again to pick Lisa up from work at ten. She apparently said she'd ride the bus to Darcy's, but Ryan doesn't want her waiting on a dark corner."

"That's very kind of him. I'm glad she has him looking out for her."

"Are *you* okay? Ryan didn't want to talk about why Lisa's so upset. Whatever happened seems to have matured him. We even managed to discuss his mother. He remembers a lot of her erratic behavior, and apologized for always blaming me."

"That's wonderful, Grant. I hope Lisa will give me the same chance. I had no clue, until Jordan mentioned it, that Lisa pretended her father left us for some important government job. How will she believe me when I tell her he was never able to keep any job for more than a few weeks?"

"I'm not the best person to give advice, but it might be best if you let Lisa cool down before you try talking to her. She probably won't listen if she's still angry."

"You don't think I should tell her what I went through with Jack?"

"I can only speak from my experience. It suited Ryan to blame me. I expected a smart kid like him could see that there are two sides to every issue. Although, in our case, I kept a lot from him."

"I do that, too. Darcy has a rotten ex. She's complained about him to me a lot. Jordan said he and

Lisa heard some of that. Lisa came away thinking I wasn't being fair to her dad."

"Should you let Lisa stay at Darcy's if that's what the atmosphere's like?"

"Darcy's a good person, but she doesn't hold back her feelings. She tends to be harsh with her ex. No gray areas for her. And I can't deny that sometimes I've let her bring that out in me, too. I honestly didn't know the kids were listening."

"You have legitimate reasons for being angry at Jack. The trick will be getting Lisa to understand."

"Difficult if she thinks he's the victim, not me."

"And it'll be impossible if she continues to shut you out of her life. Rebecca, I think we should include her in any future plans, even if she keeps living with Darcy for a while. Like, if we take the other kids out to eat, invite Lisa. The same goes for day trips. It'll make her stay in the family loop—even if all she does is say no."

"Thank you, Grant. That makes a lot of sense."

"I'm glad. Ryan thinks I've mellowed since I met you. So, why don't we get started and set up our first group outing?"

"You mean so Lisa has to choose to go along or be left out?"

"Exactly. After lunch today, Brandy and I talked about visiting the Alamo, and then having dinner on the River Walk. Next Sunday? Or we could make it lunch, if Lisa has to work at the Tumbleweed. We could even take the boys if Darcy needs her to babysit."

"You've got to be kidding. They're a handful."

"Hey, I'm just trying to cover all the bases."

"Will Ryan join us, do you think? Otherwise it won't work."

"Her moving out bothered him, Rebecca. He's very worried about her, so yes, I'd say he'll be there, as long as we explain that it's important."

"All right, it's a date. I'll call Darcy and have her pass the invitation on to Lisa. Or Ryan can. You're sure he's picking her up tonight?"

"Did you hear yourself? Remember when you demanded I convince Ryan to stop seeing Lisa?" Grant teased.

"I know. Things have changed, and Lisa needs a friend. I've been cut off from my family, Grant. I know how badly I needed…someone. It's good Lisa has Ryan. He may not want to be like you, but he *is* compassionate. And you have to give his mother credit, too. She had her problems, but she obviously did something right with him."

"Teresa had good qualities, as I told Ryan. She and I just…weren't meant to be together. We were trying to fix a relationship that couldn't be fixed."

"Yet, there are some happy memories to share with your kids. I need to remember to pass a few of my own on to Lisa and Jordan. Growing up in our community, Jack worked hard. He used to lift the heavy lugs of fruit onto the sorting tables so I wouldn't hurt my back. He just didn't have strong role models—his father was quite abusive."

"Do you ever wish you could go back and do things differently?"

"Sometimes. A counselor at the women's shelter said something that stuck with me. She said not to waste valuable energy regretting things that have already happened. Keep your eyes on the future. That's the only way to shape change."

"It's a good philosophy. I may borrow it to pass on to my kids."

"Feel free. Anyway, I'd better go see what Jordan is up to. I'm sure he's not doing his laundry." She laughed. "I'll bet Lisa didn't take her dirty clothes with her. I'll wash them, and that will give me an excuse to drop by Darcy's tomorrow to see Lisa. You know, keep channels open."

"Maybe make it the day after. Ryan said there's a home baseball game tomorrow after school. If Lisa is babysitting Darcy's boys, they'll be there."

"How much longer does baseball season last? I should know, but I just don't have time to pay attention to sports."

"Another couple of months to go. I'll get the schedule so you can post the home games on your calendar."

"Good heavens, Grant. I hope Lisa is back home before a couple of months."

"I hope so, for your sake, too. But even if she isn't, what's to stop the rest of us from going to cheer for the home team?"

"I didn't get the impression that Ryan was very

pleased when you and Brandy showed up at one of his games."

"I'll run it by him first."

"It's awfully nice having you look out for my interests. This is the first time I haven't had to handle the crappy parts alone. Not that I plan to make a habit of crying on your shoulder."

"My shoulders are available anytime, Rebecca."

There was a pause while Rebecca remembered the solid comfort of his bare shoulder under her cheek.

Grant cleared his throat, and she knew his thoughts had drifted back to their interlude, too.

"I really have to go. Bye, Grant."

Before either of them could find a reason not to, Rebecca slid her phone quietly into its cradle. She lingered with her hand on the receiver.

"What are you smiling about?" Jordan asked as he bounded into the kitchen. "Was that Lisa?"

"No, it was Grant," she said briskly. "Ryan drove Lisa to work and he's picking her up after her shift—to make sure she gets to Darcy's safely."

"And that makes you happy? I thought you didn't want her hanging around Ryan."

Closing her eyes, Rebecca massaged her temples. "Jordan, I still want Lisa to concentrate on her schoolwork so she can get a scholarship. But maybe I can give a little in other areas."

"Huh? Since when?" Jordan went to the fridge. "I should have grabbed a second hamburger at lunch. I'm still hungry."

Rebecca chuckled. There was nothing like a starving teenage boy to bring her back to reality. "There's cheese and bread in the fridge. Make a grilled cheese sandwich if you want. I'm going to toss in a load of laundry. Jordan, I'll work things out with your sister. Don't you worry."

"So, is it okay if I talk to her at school?"

"Of course. Lisa's angry at me, not you. We just have to do our best to keep the lines of communication open. Which reminds me, Grant would like the six of us to tour the Alamo next Sunday and eat out. Lisa may say no, but we can work around her schedule."

"Cool. The Alamo's awesome. I only went once with my fourth-grade class."

"I've never been. We owe Grant for shaking me out of my rut."

"I'll say. We never used to do anything fun, because you either had to work, or we had chores at home."

"Jordan, I'm sorry. I should've tried harder to make time. Just so you know, our responsibilities haven't changed. It means cramming more into fewer hours, that's all. I'll yell when I put my load in the dryer, and you can use the washer. Keep your music down, though. I need to call Darcy back."

"Maybe chores won't be such a pain if we have other stuff to look forward to on weekends. It's what I tried to tell you a few weeks ago about Lisa not working less hard at school if you let her have a social life." Jordan stuck his head in the fridge and dug around for the cheese.

As Rebecca sorted clothes in the laundry room, she was forced to admit that she'd let her life and the lives of her children stagnate.

She attempted to explain that later when she talked to Darcy. "I owe Grant for showing me that I have options."

Her friend scoffed. "How do you know he's not manipulating you?"

"What reason would he have for doing that?"

"Gee, maybe he needs a woman to cook, clean, take care of his little girl and warm his bed. Lisa seems to think he's up to something, and I have to agree with her. Do you really trust him?"

"Lisa doesn't know Grant. Nor do you, Darcy. He and Lisa met for two minutes, if that, before she flipped and stormed out."

"Rebecca, the guy's own son stood right here while she was crying her eyes out. He didn't argue with anything she said."

"Then they're both wrong. Grant hired house-keepers and nannies in Germany. He could do the same here if that's what he wanted."

"Which leaves my sex theory, unless the guy was screwing his housekeeper."

Rebecca couldn't contain a strangled sound.

"Did you hang up?"

"I'm here," Rebecca said. "It's plain you've decided to side with Lisa."

"That's so not fair. You're like the sister I never had, Rebecca, and I love Lisa like she was my own kid. I hate seeing you two at odds. And this new guy is causing trouble in your lives. Rebecca, you were a rock for me when Kevin pulled his crap. All I'm saying is go slow."

"I know your heart's in the right place, Darcy. I'm just upset about Lisa running away. It never occurred to me that one of my kids would be that unhappy. And it's my fault for not being honest with them about Jack. Please tell Lisa I love her. That's something my parents never said. While I may not agree with some of Lisa's choices, I love her unconditionally."

"I'll tell her. You've been a shining example for Lisa. She's a great kid. Give her time, she'll come around."

"I hope so. And, Darcy, I wish you'd give Grant a chance, too. I know you'll like him. Not all men are like Kevin and Jack. Grant Lane is one of the good ones."

"Well, from what I saw of him at the Tumbleweed, he's purty enough to be a keeper," Darcy drawled in exaggerated Texas fashion. "I promise, if he treats you right, I'll try to like him."

"Thanks." Rebecca hung up a minute later feeling infinitely better than she had. Darcy was right. Lisa was a great kid. Rebecca put her clothes in the dryer with renewed confidence that her daughter would do the right thing.

SUNDAY, a full week later, as Rebecca stood aside outside the adobe walls of the Alamo waiting for Grant, who stood in line to purchase tickets, her belief in her daughter's good sense had waned.

Jordan, Brandy and Ryan were huddled near the huge carved doors of the old mission, pointing out bullet holes still visible in the weathered wood. The kids were excited by the prospect of touring the historic site. Only Lisa had refused to join them. She still wouldn't speak to Rebecca, period. Jordan saw her at school, but reported that she never said anything of importance.

Rebecca watched Grant step away from the ticket window and walk to where she held their place in line to enter the gate. He was tall and lithe, and today—he was hers.

Or not, she mused as the kids swarmed him. He passed them each a ticket and handed Jordan a map. Then Grant and Ryan talked earnestly for another minute. Finally Grant pointed to his watch and the three kids took off.

Surprised, Rebecca shouldered her way through a group of Japanese visitors queuing up for a guided tour.

"Aren't we going with them?" she asked, reaching Grant at last.

"They want to do their own thing. The boys are going to keep tabs on Brandy. According to the map, the area inside the plaza isn't large."

"That's what Jordan said."

"Ryan's history teacher suggested he see the docudrama at the IMAX Theater behind the Alamo when he finishes the tour here. Jordan was moderately interested in going, but Brandy's not keen. She pointed out that the historic sites in Germany were a lot older and had more statues."

"Do you want to go to the theater with the boys? Brandy and I can wander through craft shops until it's over."

"I could join them, I guess," Grant said, lacking enthusiasm. "I've missed you, Rebecca. I hoped we could spend all day together, but it would be good to have some time with Ryan. I'm surprised he agreed to come, especially after Lisa refused. I take it nothing's changed between you two."

"Not a thing." Rebecca stopped walking as Grant paused to look at a cannon. "Darcy's house is a bit chaotic with her four boys. I didn't think Lisa would last two days, let alone a full week."

"My house got more chaotic as of Tuesday. I told you that Brandy's been bugging me for a puppy. She wanted a shih tzu, but Ryan wanted a bigger dog. I put them off, saying they had to agree on a breed first. Monday, we visited the Humane Society animal shelter—only to look. We went back Tuesday and brought home a year-old schnauzer named York."

"So where does chaos come in?"

"From the kids both wanting York to sleep in their room. Ryan gave in once I pointed out he'd be going off to college soon, which would be disruptive to the dog."

"At least you and Ryan seem to be getting along better."

"Sometimes. We had words when I first invited him to the Alamo with us. I maybe shouldn't tell you, but he said Lisa thinks we're trying to keep them apart by making it seem like they'll be stepbrother and –sister one day."

Rebecca stumbled, almost falling against the side of a covered wagon. Grant caught her, and didn't immediately let her go. He stood, looking earnestly into her eyes while running his hands up and down her arms.

"You assured me the night they went to the dance that Ryan said they were just friends," Rebecca said uneasily.

"He did. But I guess there are girls at school giving Lisa a hard time. Since you and I have been out in public together, I guess they're afraid word will get out and foil their pretense of going steady."

"But Lisa knows better. About us, I mean. We're just friends, too. If I live to be a hundred, I'll never understand why people spread rumors."

Grant arched an eyebrow at her depiction of their relationship. But, because she started walking again, he shrugged. "Beats me why people gossip. Look, here come the kids. If you've seen enough of the Alamo, shall we move on?"

"This place is really cool," Jordan exclaimed.

"Ryan picked up a brochure on a play or a film he's gonna see at the IMAX. Do you think I could use anything from the film in Texas culture class?" He aimed the question at Grant, not Rebecca. It troubled her, until she remembered that she'd wanted Grant and Jordan to bond. Her son lacked a man's viewpoint.

Grant read the brochure. "I don't think it could hurt, Jordan, and you might even be able to write something about it for extra credit if your teacher agrees. It sounds interesting. Do you mind if I join you guys?"

"I don't," Jordan shot back. "So, Mom, are you coming, too?"

She shook her head. "Brandy, I thought you and I could check out the craft stores across the street instead."

"Goody, goody!" Brandy clapped her hands. "But, Daddy, will York be okay if we leave him home alone so long?"

"He'll be fine," Grant assured her, smiling indulgently. "We left him plenty of water. He's gated in the laundry room where he has blankets if he wants to nap."

"Who's York?" Jordan asked. Ryan and Brandy both rushed to tell him about their latest acquisition.

"I wish I had a dog," Jordan said.

Brandy clutched his arm. "You can share York if you'd like. Daddy said Ryan's going off to college soon."

"Hey, I'll come home at breaks, so don't be

giving away my stake in our dog. I've wanted one for a long time, too, but Dad never listened to me."

Grant frowned. "The first I heard of anyone wanting a dog was when Brandy mentioned her friend's shih tzu."

"I begged Mom for a German shepherd when I was little," Ryan said. "She told me you wouldn't let us have an animal because dogs slobber germs."

Grant let the accusation go. He didn't want to get into an argument today. But he could've told his son that Teresa was the one obsessed with germs. Since she'd died of an infection, maybe she had reason.

"My mom said dogs cost too much to feed and take to the vet and stuff." Jordan glanced up guiltily, as if afraid he'd revealed a flaw in his mother.

"They aren't cheap." Grant and Rebecca spoke together, making them laugh. Without thinking, each made a fist, then bumped knuckles and tugged on each other's pinkie finger. Seeing the kids' confused expressions, Grant said, "It's a generational thing. Everyone our age did that growing up."

Even with the explanation, Ryan looked uncomfortable. "So stop acting like you're still kids, already."

"You'd better go to the theater, Grant," Rebecca said in a stage whisper. "Before Ryan freaks out about the way we old folk are acting."

Grant grinned. "What's the big deal, Ryan? It's a harmless practice. Obviously Rebecca thinks so, too," he said, nudging her playfully.

She nudged him back, and Ryan again muttered

how dumb it looked, having people their age carrying on in public.

"Want to show my son we're still young at heart, Becca? We'll sit in the back row and neck," Grant teased.

"That would be a new one. I never went to a movie as a teenager, let alone necked in one."

"Eww." Ryan rolled his eyes. Even Jordan gagged.

"Yuck, Mom!"

Rebecca's smile spread. "Don't blame me. Grant made the suggestion."

"Anyway," Grant said, "boys, shall we go? Rebecca, where do you want to meet? Is there a good restaurant near here?"

"We should go to the Tumbleweed and make Lisa wait on us," Jordan joked.

Ryan nixed that. "She might refuse. Do you want her to get into trouble?"

"Ryan, do you really think she's still that angry?"

Ryan wouldn't meet Rebecca's eyes. He abruptly turned and headed for the IMAX.

Rebecca touched Grant's arm when he moved to follow his son. She chased after Ryan herself and caught up to him as he exited the bullet-riddled doors the kids had examined earlier. "Ryan, I have the feeling something more is bothering you. Has Lisa said anything about coming home?"

"No, nothing like that. I should keep my nose out of this, Mrs. Geroux. Except…after what you said at my house last week about Mr. Geroux, I'm worried, okay? Lisa admitted that she's tried a few times in the past to find her dad. She didn't know he was in prison. Neither did I. And well, she was floundering around on the Internet, so I gave her some tips. I wouldn't have if I'd known the truth. Thing is, she was on MySpace the other day and found some guy she thinks is her dad."

"What?" Rebecca's yelp stopped passersby. "Oh my God. I can't believe it. Has she contacted him? What if he tracks her down?" In her panic, Rebecca clutched the front of Ryan's shirt.

"I set her up with a blind before she started e-mailing. And I told her to be careful. After what you said Sunday, I've tried to get her to stop. Now she's mad at me," he explained, trying to escape Rebecca's grip.

Grant ran up and came between the tense pair. "All right, you two. What's the problem? Rebecca, was Ryan rude?"

"No, no, Grant," she said, biting her lower lip. "It's not his fault. Thank you for trying to talk to Lisa, Ryan. Sorry if I wrinkled your shirt. I'll…uh…I'll handle her from here on out."

Grant darted a quick glance back at the younger kids, who were lagging behind. "Ryan, perhaps you can update me on the way over to the theater. We need to go, or we'll miss the opening. That is, if we're still going." He looked from one to the other. "Rebecca, you're awfully pale."

Ryan shifted his weight, clearly leaving the decision to Rebecca.

"Go to the movie. I need time to…think." She took a deep breath.

Ryan nodded and strode off.

"Where's Ryan going?" Jordan asked as he and Brandy finally caught up. "Aren't you coming to the movie, Grant? Hey, Ryan! Wait up!" Jordan hollered. "Mom, is it still okay if I go to the IMAX?"

"Yes. But, Grant, go on with the boys. You really don't need to worry about what Ryan told me. Like I said, I just need time to think before I confront Lisa." She shooed him away, not wanting to ruin his day with his son.

Grant looked perplexed, but gently brushed his knuckles across her cheek. "We'll talk later. You ladies have fun shopping."

He started off after the boys, but stopped when Brandy ran up to him, saying, "Daddy, I can't shop without money."

"How much do you need, sweetheart?" He pulled out his wallet.

She shrugged. "I've never shopped here before. I don't know what I might want to buy."

"Spoken like a true shopaholic," Grant said, yanking one of her curls. He peeled off two twenties and passed them to Rebecca, who glanced at the amount in dismay. "I'd appreciate it if you'd supervise and don't let her spend it all on junk food. Hey, guys," he yelled at the fast-departing boys. "If you don't want to pay your own way into the theater, wait up."

"Grant, this is a lot of cash for a kid," Rebecca said, but he was already trotting off. He didn't slow down, so she folded the money and tucked it in her pocket.

"What kind of crafts do they have?" Brandy asked when they reached the corner crosswalk. "One of my friends' mom is teaching her to knit. Do you knit?"

"I used to. I haven't had time in years." Rebecca answered Brandy, but her mind was on the dilemma with Lisa. Surely the authorities at state prisons wouldn't let an inmate have a Web site. If so, who *was* Lisa e-mailing? Rebecca shivered. She'd heard how easy it was for predators to connect with kids via the Internet. She wasn't paying for Internet service, which meant Lisa must be. No wonder she'd quit contributing to her college fund. Rebecca's biggest concern had always been that Jack would find them. She'd never dreamed that her children would try to locate *him*. Because the prospect frightened her, she focused on the girl skipping along at her side.

"We'll see pottery shops, local wood carvers, all kinds of clothing and jewelry. Darcy bought a really pretty hair barrette last time she came here. Abalone shell with inlaid flowers and leaves in mother-of-pearl. Something like that would look nice in your hair, Brandy."

"I like shells, but my nanny had pearls I wasn't allowed to touch. One day I tried them on and she slapped me. Ryan told her to never do that again or he'd get her fired. I don't think I'll buy pearls."

"Honey, that's terrible. I'll tell you what, we'll only buy things that make us happy."

"Did you ever slap Lisa or Jordan?"

"Never. They got told no a lot, though. Jordan learned to read the clock because he had so many time-outs."

Brandy smiled at that. "I hope you marry Daddy. Do you think maybe you will?"

Rebecca had nearly forgotten how blunt children could be. "I like your daddy, Brandy. And he likes me. Liking each other is a place to begin a relationship," Rebecca said, leading the way into one shop. "We haven't known each other long enough to talk marriage, sweetie."

"You're not going to marry him?" Brandy pouted.

"He hasn't asked me." Rebecca steered the girl toward some hand-carved, brightly painted parrots.

Brandy brightened. "Can I tell him I want him to ask you?"

Rebecca groaned inwardly. "People have to be in love to get married, and sometimes that develops slowly."

"Sometimes doesn't mean always. Doesn't it sometimes explode real fast? You know, like the salad bowl you dropped? Daddy didn't get mad at you for spilling. He asked first if you were hurt. I think that means he loves you."

Rebecca's head spun. She opened her mouth to

deny Brandy's reasoning, but the girl had already moved on to a stall where a girl about her age was having her hair braided. "That's called cornrowing," she murmured to Brandy.

"Oh, I want that done, please. Unless it costs more than what Daddy gave me."

"Twenty dollars," the woman said in heavily accented English. Brandy moved closer to Rebecca, who instinctively bargained. "Will you take fifteen?"

The woman sighed and glanced behind her. Rebecca noticed three small girls, dark-eyed clones of the woman who stood on a bare cement floor, her legs swollen. Rebecca could braid Brandy's hair for nothing, but she could tell this woman needed every cent she earned. Rebecca had been in her shoes once.

"Twenty," she agreed, and gave a brief hug to Brandy, who only knew she wanted the braiding done.

Rebecca waited outside the booth. This hairdresser's eyes were old beyond her years. Her shoulders had a permanent slump. Rebecca recognized that feeling, too. It was precisely why she wanted her daughter to go to college.

The longer Rebecca studied the weary mother, the more she realized that she needed to be completely honest with her kids about Jack. Especially Lisa. Then they would both understand the folly of wanting to find their dad. It was more than foolish. It was dangerous.

CHAPTER TEN

BRANDY BOUNCED along beside Rebecca, the colorful beads attached to the ends of her braids clinking musically. The girl's happy smile made Rebecca regret that she'd never had the money or the time to take Lisa shopping just for fun. Necessities had always come first.

"Where should we go next, Rebecca?"

"We only have fifteen minutes until we have to meet your dad and the boys. If you want to buy him and Ryan those San Antonio Spurs T-shirts, we'd better turn back now."

"They were two for twenty dollars. That's all the money I have left. I won't be able to buy anything for you and Jordan."

"We have tax here, too, don't forget," Rebecca said.

"Daddy didn't give me enough money, but you can give me more, right?"

"Forty dollars is plenty. It's very sweet of you to think of us, Brandy, but it's okay for you to buy just for your family."

The girl slipped her hand into Rebecca's. "I had

the best time today. Did you hear the clerk at the candle shop say the candle I lit was a wishing flame? Know what I wished? That we'd all be a family," she said, not giving Rebecca a chance to guess.

"Honey, wishes don't always come true," Rebecca cautioned. "But you know that even if…we merged our families, most days would be ordinary."

"But if you lived with us, you'd understand girl stuff."

"Lisa would say I'm not very good at that."

"She's silly to be mad. I heard Ryan tell her on the phone to get over it. Oh, there's the shirt shop. I know, I'll buy Ryan and Jordan shirts."

The shirts didn't look well made. "You could save your money for another shopping spree," Rebecca suggested.

"Daddy gave it to me for today." Brandy sifted through a stack. "What sizes should I get?"

"I'll have to guess at Ryan's. Look at these. Maybe he'd rather have a Texas Rangers shirt since he plays baseball."

"Spurs for Jordan and Rangers for Ryan. That's a great idea, Rebecca. Thanks."

Brandy paid for her purchases, needing and expecting Rebecca to fork over the tax. That's when Rebecca started to worry that Grant wouldn't approve of how she'd let his daughter spend his money. She didn't realize she'd muttered as much out loud until Brandy said, "If you lived with us, Daddy would give you all the money you wanted, too."

They rounded a corner then and saw Grant and the boys walking toward them. Brandy took off running. Rebecca heard Grant exclaim, "Whoa! Who's this island girl?"

"*Daddy*. Do you like my hair? I got to pick the beads myself. But I didn't have enough money to buy you anything. I didn't have any money left after I bought shirts for Ryan and Jordan. Rebecca had to give me extra." Brandy pulled the T-shirts out of the bag as Rebecca joined them.

Jordan accepted the shirt Brandy handed him. "Hey, cool. I'm a big Spurs fan. Thanks, Brandy, but it's not even my birthday, or Christmas."

"Yeah, thanks. The Rangers are awesome." Ryan held the shirt across his chest. "Looks like it'll fit, too."

"Rebecca helped me with sizes. But, Daddy, she's worried 'cause I spent all the money you gave me, plus some of hers."

Grant turned back to Rebecca. "What do I owe you? And don't worry about Brandy spending the money—that's why I gave it to her."

"I only paid the tax on the shirts. But, Grant, forty bucks is too much for any eleven-year-old to spend on frivolous things like braids and novelty shirts. At least the woman who braided Brandy's hair had three little girls to feed."

"Brandy obviously loves her hair, so it was well worth it. I think it was generous of her to spend some on the boys, too, instead of all on herself."

Grant just didn't get it. "Yes, but you know I could've done the braids for free."

"You can braid like this?" Brandy gazed at Rebecca in awe. "Daddy, if they come live with us, you'd give her and Jordan plenty of money, wouldn't you?"

The boys had walked on ahead. Grant set a hand on Rebecca's waist. "Now that's tempting." The grin faded when Rebecca's back stiffened and he realized Brandy wasn't joking. "Honey, why would you think Rebecca would live with us?" To Rebecca he whispered, "Did I miss something? I hope she didn't make assumptions, like proposing I hire you to cook and keep our house. Brandy's used to having hired help."

"Nothing like that, Grant. It's just…I'm afraid money will always divide us. We think about it so differently. Jordan said it all—my kids never get 'just because' gifts."

Grant whipped out his wallet, thumbed out a pair of ones and tucked them in her hand. She wadded them up and shoved them in her pocket. He didn't owe her that much, but his cavalier attitude irritated Rebecca, especially when he said, "You're the only one who has a problem with the money situation. I keep trying to help you, but you won't let me. It's not a barrier unless you want it to be."

Brandy inserted her body between them, and she grasped their hands. "My teacher said it's normal for parents to argue sometimes, but it doesn't mean they don't love each other. So see, you guys are practically a family already. Except we don't live in the same house. I like our house. So does York. But to be fair we have to visit Rebecca and Jordan's home before we vote. My teacher said families who make important decisions by voting are happiest. I want us to be happy, don't you?" She smiled at her dad.

Grant tugged his earlobe. "Brandy, you're rushing things. But it so happens, I planned to surprise Rebecca this afternoon. In the car I have a brand-new garbage disposal to replace her broken one. Ryan, Jordan and I have arranged to swap the two right after we grab a bite to eat, so we'll see her house then."

"You didn't tell me that," Rebecca sputtered.

Grant tapped the tip of her nose with his forefinger. "That's why I called it a surprise."

Rebecca's protest fizzled on her tongue, and she felt a strange emotion building inside. She was loath to call it love.

"Thank you, Grant," she said perfunctorily. "It's a wonderful surprise. But rather than you buying us lunch, let me fix a meal at my house as partial payment," she said as Grant unlocked the car and they took their seats.

"Rebecca! What did I just say? Accept the gift. There are no strings. With three men and tools spread all over your kitchen floor, how could you possibly cook?"

"Right. My kitchen is tiny," she admitted.

Ryan butted in. "We could get takeout from one of the chicken places. We have tons of menus at home. While Brandy collects York, Jordan and I can call the order in."

Rebecca held her tongue and left that up to Grant. She listened while Ryan and Brandy argued over which place served the best chicken. Grant offered a third opinion. At that point Brandy reached through the bucket seats and poked Jordan, who sat next to Ryan. "We all like different spots. You break the tie."

"I don't know any of those restaurants. We always eat at home."

"Always?" Ryan couldn't hide his surprise.

Grant turned onto their street. "It's probably healthier that way."

"Not if you ask Lisa," Jordan put in. "She nags Mom because she fixes pasta too much, and other stuff with lots of carbs. Lisa bitch…uh…gripes." He shot a sidelong apology to Brandy for slipping with his language.

"Lisa especially dislikes a cookbook you have called *101 Ways to Fix Hamburger,* Mrs. G.," Ryan added.

"Enough. It's human nature to want what you don't have," Grant declared, stopping in their driveway. "We eat takeout too often. Brandy would rather we cooked at home. Lisa and Jordan might like to get takeout once in a while."

"Lisa's always wanted whatever we can't afford." Rebecca gave an inelegant snort. "She'd better get a good education and a good job so she can pay for it herself."

"Lisa needs more. Other girls spent a fortune on clothes for the Spring Fling. Lisa had to make do with what she had," Ryan stated.

Grant stepped in. "Ryan, Rebecca does the best she can. There are more important things than clothes, you know. Becca, he didn't mean anything by that. He's a kid."

"I know some things," Ryan growled, climbing out of the SUV. "I already told Mrs. Geroux that Lisa's trying to find her dad on the Internet. If anyone cares to know why she's looking, it's because she thinks dads have more money and fewer rules than moms." Slamming the car door, Ryan hurried toward the house.

Half out of his seat, Jordan hesitated. "Mom, is that true? Can Lisa find Dad? Is that even safe?"

Brandy had yet to wiggle her way out of the car. Grant saw her and did his best to distract her. "Brandy, hon, why don't you show Jordan your dog? Do you remember where I put the travel bag we bought to carry York's food and water? Get it ready to go, then you kids order chicken to pick up on our way to Rebecca's."

Rebecca gave Grant's hand a grateful squeeze. "Jordan," she said, "I know you're worried about your sister. We'll talk about it more when we have time. I just…well, I can't imagine your father using a computer."

Relieved, Jordan jumped from the vehicle, then helped Brandy down. They ran off, leaving Grant and Rebecca alone in the SUV.

"Is that what Ryan told you at the Alamo? No wonder you looked so shocked. He wouldn't tell me anything."

"Don't be mad at him, Grant. I'm glad he told me or I'd never have known. I'm sure Darcy has no idea what Lisa's doing on the Internet. The kids and I bought the laptop a year ago, so they could do their homework. Lisa took it with her. Ryan said she found a Web site she thinks belongs to Jack, and she's been e-mailing him anonymously. Say it's not even Jack. That's scary, too. Inmates wouldn't be allowed to have Web sites, would they?"

"You'd be surprised. I know a retired air force intelligence officer who has built a solid business tracking creeps, many who run scams from behind bars. You shouldn't have given your kids unsupervised access to the Web."

"I didn't. Lisa must have used her own money."

"Does she have a credit card? Most sites ask for payment online."

"That's a relief. Lisa doesn't have a credit card. Neither does Darcy, so she can't get through that way. Darcy canceled hers after Kevin ran up a bunch of bills and left her to pay them."

"He sounds like a real ass."

"To say the least. I should mention that Darcy warned me not to trust you. She's bitter. She took

Kevin at his word once, and let him back into her life. He cheated yet again, and drained their bank account, too. After leaving her pregnant with the twins."

"Okay, so she's not likely to help Lisa find your ex."

"No, but Lisa's sharp. I've seen her research material online for school papers at the library. I'm always amazed. She can find anything."

"Does Lisa know where he is? What state has him locked up?"

"Oregon. She knows I grew up there, so it's not a stretch to connect that with Jack."

"Is Jack his legal name, or is it John?"

"John. He's John Samuel Geroux. Strong Biblical names like everyone else in our order. Do you think she'll have trouble finding him as Jack?"

"I hope so." Grant tilted Rebecca's face up with both hands, then kissed her tenderly.

"What if the kids are watching?" she murmured breathlessly when the kiss ended.

"I don't care. I want to erase your memories of living with that man, and the hard times you went through afterward."

"I survived. But I'd walk barefoot over hot coals to keep Lisa and Jordan away from him. Maybe while you guys are installing the disposal I'll drive over and visit Lisa. I can come right out and tell her I know she's looking for her father."

"Won't she be furious with Ryan? She'll know immediately who told you. Arc you sure you want to cut off your only source of information?"

"You're right, Grant. I should've thought of that. But how can I make her stop? She's e-mailing some strange man. That's bad even if it turns out not to be Jack. Grant, I'm so stunned. I thought she was smarter than that."

"Sweetheart, this has nothing to do with being smart. It's emotional. She's a kid who wants a father."

"Okay, but if I don't confront her, what should I do?"

"For starters let me bring my laptop to your house. After we eat, and once the boys and I install the disposal, we can send them to a movie. That will give us a chance to do some searching of our own."

"What happens if he's easy to find?"

"Let's not worry about that yet. I'm willing to give you any help you need to keep her safe. If you'll accept it."

Rebecca brushed the back of her hand over Grant's angular jaw. "You can probably tell it's not easy for me to give up even a smidgen of control. But it seems to be getting easier with time. I really appreciate you sharing this burden with me."

His hand cupped hers briefly before he carried her fingers to his lips. The front door slammed, and Rebecca jerked away. "It's Brandy. She's got the dog and Jordan has the travel pack," she said, peering out the windshield.

Grant reluctantly let go of her. "I'll go see what's keeping Ryan." He slipped out, and the next thing

Rebecca knew, she was being kissed by the slobbery tongue of a schnauzer.

"Aren't you the friendly sort," she exclaimed, laughing as she tried to wipe her chin and escape the dog's enthusiastic greeting.

Jordan dumped the travel bag in the SUV and boosted Brandy up so that she could corral her rambunctious pet. "York's just glad to be out of the laundry room. Brandy, keep a tighter hold of his leash," he ordered. "Not everyone likes dog drool on their face. Remember what Ryan said."

"Rebecca's laughing, so she doesn't mind," Brandy countered. "And Ryan thinks he knows everything, just 'cause he's older than me."

Rebecca noticed that even after repeatedly offering York doggy treats, Brandy failed to coax him into the backseat with her.

"I've never had a dog, Brandy, but maybe you shouldn't give York treats until he does what you want. For instance, if he follows you to the backseat, then reward him."

"Right…that's what the book my friend gave me says. I should've remembered." Brandy hugged the wiggling dog, and then burst into tears.

"Honey, what is it?" Rebecca released her seat belt and climbed into the narrow passage between the seats.

"I'm a bad pet owner. I promised Daddy I'd teach York manners, but he won't listen to me."

"It takes patience, Brandy. It's not going to happen immediately."

"I want York to behave now so you'll come live with us. If he's naughty, you won't want to be part of our family."

At a loss for words, Rebecca pulled a tissue out of her pocket, and urged the girl to wipe her face.

Jordan looked annoyed. "Mom, Ryan and I both told Brandy that we aren't going to be a family anytime soon. We're not, are we? You'd ask Lisa and me first... right?"

Rebecca felt herself torn between Jordan and Brandy. "Kids, the only plan we have today is to pick up chicken and take it to our house to eat. After that, Grant, Ryan and Jordan will replace the broken disposal. That's it. Speaking of Grant and Ryan, where are they?"

Brandy blotted her eyes. "Ryan's ordering our food and Daddy went to find his toolbox."

"Here they come." Jordan pointed toward the garage.

Fighting a headache, Rebecca returned to her seat.

York erupted in a series of high-pitched yips the minute Grant popped the back hatch to set his toolbox and laptop inside. "Easy, boy. That's a good watchdog, but we're part of your family."

Woofing low in his throat, the schnauzer put his paws on the back of Ryan's seat, and sniffed the teen's ear. "Hey, your nose is cold," Ryan said, shrinking away from the dog's reach. "Colonel, can

Jordan and I change the disposal by ourselves? I replaced one in our base rental by myself. You weren't around."

"I'll consider it, Ryan, if you quit calling me Colonel. If Dad is too much to handle, I'll settle for Grant."

Ryan slumped in his seat. Rebecca could see his mutinous expression in the mirror. "I'm here, aren't I? Isn't that enough?" he snapped.

Rebecca reached across the console and gave Grant's knee a warning pat. "Does your dad know which restaurant to stop at?" she asked Ryan.

All three kids sang out the name.

Grant drove straight there. The minute he brought the bags of food into the vehicle, York was enticed by the aroma. It took all three kids to keep him in the backseat for the short drive to the Geroux home.

"Gosh, your house is squirty," Brandy said after they exited the SUV and tramped into Rebecca's compact kitchen. Ryan was about to take York for a turn around the yard, but couldn't resist harassing his sister. "Brandy, honestly, you're such a dork."

"I am not!"

"Are, too."

"Hey, hey, kids!" Grant paused in the act of depositing food cartons on the kitchen counter. "Ryan, go take the dog out. Brandy, apologize to Rebecca. It was a thoughtless comment."

Brandy sobbed again. York didn't like hearing her cry. He bounded the length of his leash, barking nonstop as Ryan led him out the back door. The shrill noise echoed in the compact kitchen.

Rebecca handed Jordan a stack of plates. "Will you set the table?" Crossing to the sniffing child, she bent to Brandy's level. "Brandy, it's okay that you said my house is squirty. It is." Rebecca straightened and addressed Grant. "Why make her apologize for telling the truth?"

Grant threw up his hands. "Your house, your call. Where shall I set up York's food and water?" he asked as Ryan returned with the dog.

Scanning the room, Rebecca realized there was no good place. Jordan came to her rescue. "The laundry room isn't big, but at least it's tile so he won't spill on the carpet."

Rebecca nodded her approval. "You and Brandy take care of that, please. Then wash your hands and come to the table."

"Mom, we only have four chairs, and there's five of us. If we're careful, can we kids watch TV in the living room while we eat?" Jordan nudged the silent Ryan. "The Rangers are playing the Angels."

Ryan perked up, and high-fived Jordan.

Rebecca saw Brandy's face fall. "If you don't want to watch the game, Brandy, you may join your father and me at the table."

"I wish Lisa was here." Brandy pouted.

"So do I," Rebecca said with a tremor in her voice. "I miss her."

Ryan helped himself to a drumstick. "Lisa doesn't like living at Darcy's."

"Then for heaven's sake, why doesn't she come home?" Rebecca couldn't contain her exasperation.

"I don't know if I should say. She's already mad at me."

"Now that you've started," Grant said, "don't hold back."

Ryan paused, then relented. "When we met, Lisa and I found we had a lot in common. We're both oldest kids of a single parent who wasn't home much. We both had questions about our folks' marriages. The other night, the colonel…my dad answered some of mine," Ryan admitted. "Lisa, though, is more confused than ever. I got to know both my mom and dad. Lisa doesn't remember her father, so she made stuff up. It really hurt her to find out she was wrong."

Rebecca sank down in a chair. She burst out angrily, "You mean the crap about Jack being an FBI agent? That's so bogus. Oh, never mind." She waved him away. "It's not your fault. I shouldn't yell at you. Go watch your game and eat your chicken before it gets cold."

Brandy looked up from filling her plate. "If everybody here is going to act all mad, I'll go watch the game," she said, and promptly followed Jordan into the living room.

Ryan buttered a roll. "One last thing. Lisa's had years to turn her dad into a hero. I know she's struggling to process what you said about him, Mrs. G., but she's still hoping he's not as bad as you think."

Remaining on the sideline, Grant loaded two plates with food. Once Ryan joined the other kids, Grant set one in front of Rebecca and passed her a soda. Scooting his chair nearer hers, he sat down. "Maybe Lisa just needs a little more time to come around."

Rebecca fiddled with her straw. "I had the opportunity to tell her the truth a number of weeks ago when she accused me of hating men. I chickened out and said something meaningless, like 'tell me when I ever have time to date.' Then the next thing she knows, you announce that we've been dating. Then I drop the bombshell about Jack being in prison. Of course she's angry. What kid wants to hear their parent criticized?"

"None. Which is why I should be more tolerant of Ryan's issues with me. His mother fed him a line of bull."

"Luckily for you, Grant, he seems to be more accepting than Lisa."

"We're slowly making progress. And so will you." He teased her mouth with a kiss. "Tell me what I can do."

"There's not much either of us can do without letting her know that Ryan betrayed her trust. We certainly can't talk to her."

"Good point. All right, that leaves surfing the net and finding Jack ourselves."

"Can we really do that?"

"We can try. Eat up, Rebecca, then I'll get the boys started with your disposal. You and I will get started on the laptop, and I'll run through some of the search engines."

"Thank you. But what about Brandy? I'd hate to have her worry about this."

"Does Jordan have a PSP or anything like that? If he doesn't mind, Brandy could maybe play with it."

"He does have one. I'll ask." Rebecca breathed deeply and rubbed her face with both hands.

Grant slung a comforting arm around her shoulders. "Try not to make yourself sick over this. Lisa's a smart girl. You raised her, so she'd have to be. Just trust that she'll see through her father if she ever connects with him."

"You weren't kidding when you said this is emotional." She slowly dragged her hands away from her face. "Grant, without you, I wouldn't know where to begin."

"Then I shouldn't remind you that if I hadn't moved here you wouldn't be going through this."

She laid a finger over his lips. "I'd have had to tell them the truth sooner or later. Better now, and with your support."

"I'm glad you feel that way. We've both had unsupportive partners in the past. It's different between us. All we have to do is start fresh and build a better life for both our families."

"You're right. I doubt we'll ever have to deal with anything as bad as what we've been through.

Now, do you want your plate heated? Turns out I *am* hungry after all."

"Me, too," he said, handing her his plate and giving a sexy grin. "But that will have to wait until we're alone."

Rebecca felt her ears turn red. "You are so bad." She swiped a hand playfully at him after she put his plate in the microwave.

They sobered when Ryan and Jordan came back for seconds. The boys lingered to talk to Grant about the disposal while Rebecca heated their food.

"Jordan, do you have any PlayStation games that Brandy could play? Grant said he'd show me some basics on his laptop, and you boys will be busy working on the sink."

"Brandy's probably played most of what I have, but sure. If you're learning stuff about the computer, Mom, does that mean you're going to buy another one? I told Lisa I was ticked that she took ours. Hey!" He snapped his fingers. "If you're afraid she'll search for Dad on the Web, just go confiscate her laptop. You bought it. And that way I can have it back."

"I thought of that, Jordan, but Lisa uses the computer a lot for school."

"So do I," he grumbled. "She always gets first dibs."

"Because she'll go to college first. If you really need the computer, let's hope she comes home soon."

Jordan shrugged. "I sorta like not sharing a

bathroom. Lisa always had girl stuff all around the sink."

Brandy set her empty plate in the sink as Jordan complained. "Our house has loads of bathrooms," she said. "If you lived with us, everyone could have their own. Well, except your mom. She'd share with my dad, 'cause that's what parents do."

It wasn't until after the boys had started ripping out the old disposal and Brandy went happily off with her games that Rebecca realized no one had voiced a rebuttal this time to Brandy's suggestion.

"What are you smiling about?" Grant murmured. He stopped tapping keys and filtered a hand through her red hair. Their legs and shoulders touched as they bent together over the laptop.

"I'm enjoying Brandy's noisy game, and hearing Ryan explain to Jordan which wrench to use. Mostly, I love sitting here with you."

"Damn, I hate to ruin your day, Becca. Look what I found." He clicked on a link to a blog called *Befriend an Inmate*. "I may have found Jack."

"No!" She studied the site. "That's not his picture."

"There's no rule that says a person has to be truthful on the Internet. Which is how kids get in trouble sometimes."

"That's criminal." Rebecca leaned closer, pressing her cheek to Grant's shoulder.

"I agree. Even the vilest prisoners can set up scam sites online."

Rebecca scanned more blog posts. "What a pack

of lies. If it is Jack, he claims he's in jail because his wife made false claims against him for battery. And that I—well, she—set him up to be watched by a woman cop. I never did that! Who would believe this drivel? Good Lord, did you read the comments readers have posted? Every last one expresses outrage and sympathy for him. And they're all women's names." She bolted upright. "Grant, is there any way to tell if Lisa's left any comments?"

"That's what I was looking for. I didn't see anyone with her name or initials. But it looks like he's offered to e-mail two or three of the posters privately. See here, one asked if he has kids. And later on, she asks where his family is."

"I honestly never thought it would be this easy to find him." Rebecca gnawed on her lip.

"He's cagey." Grant typed in a few more things. "Check this out. I found a second Web site."

Rebecca peered at a grainy photograph. "He's obviously older, but it could be Jack. Whoever it is doesn't mind flaunting his prison garb."

"Imagine him twenty or so years younger, twenty or so pounds lighter, and probably without his ponytail, and I bet you'd get the guy you knew."

Rebecca ran a finger over the screen. "He looks bigger. Harder. In a way, Grant, it makes me want to cry. It didn't have to be like this. Jack threw away so much."

Grant took hold of Rebecca's clenched hands. "His loss is my gain," he said.

She studied their joined hands. "Grant, I've got to make Lisa listen to me. I simply have to." They sat quietly for a minute, their temples pressed together, as if they could pass strength from one to the other.

Rebecca's telephone rang. Blinking, she slowly got up to answer it.

Jordan had crawled out from under the sink, and he got to the phone before Rebecca did. "'Lo," he said. Almost at once he covered the receiver. "Mom, it's Lisa. She's bawling, and she wants you."

Rebecca grabbed the phone. "Lisa, honey, what is it? Are you hurt? Calm down, I can't understand a word."

"Mama, I've been so stupid. Ryan warned me to stop. To cancel my e-mail account…but I didn't listen. I…" Lisa's speech was clogged with tears again. "I found Daddy. We e-mailed a bunch." Lisa was sobbing too hard to continue.

"Don't cry, sweetheart. It's okay. Tell me, what has he done or said to upset you?"

"I know I should never have gone looking. I found his blog and at first he seemed nice. I asked if he had kids. It was as if he had the blog just for me. Like he wanted to find me, too. That's what I thought when he gave me his e-mail. He showed real interest in me—in what I did, where I went to school. I was dumb and told him I was in San Antonio. Today, though, when I checked my messages, his tone had changed. He called you terrible names, like b-bitch."

"Lisa, he's behind bars. He can't touch us."

"He said he has friends who are free, and he's going to have them take care of you. He rambled for three pages, Mom. He thinks that I'll go with him when he gets out. I'm so sorry. But, Mom, I'm really scared, too." In her fear, Lisa sounded like a little girl.

Rebecca shivered. She reminded herself that she wasn't alone. She had Grant beside her, and soon Lisa would be home where she belonged. "I can't tell you how sorry I am, honey, that he said those things to you. I'll come get you right away. We should've discussed him. It's my fault, not yours. I could have saved you this."

"I tried calling Ryan's cell, but got no answer. Last week he made me mad when he said he planned to go to the Alamo with you and his dad. That's why I answered those questions from Daddy. But Ryan was right. I owe both of you a big apology." Lisa sounded calmer.

"He's here, honey. Ryan and Jordan are installing a garbage disposal."

"Really? Okay, that's something else. I know I let you think we were dating, and I wanted a boyfriend, so I'd feel like other girls. But Ryan said he just wanted us to be friends. He's just a heck of a nice guy, and I've been so bratty. How can you forgive me?"

"Lisa, I love you. Maybe I haven't said it often enough. Can Darcy get along without you? I want us all to be together."

"Darcy heard you, Mom. She's nodding."

"Ryan's dad, Brandy and Jordan are all here now. We're all behind you, Lisa. Everything's going to be fine, you'll see."

As Grant listened to Rebecca's side of the conversation, he got up and began rubbing the tension from her shoulders.

She felt love flow through his fingertips, and for the first time in a long while, believed things would be all right.

CHAPTER ELEVEN

THEY LEFT the boys to finish installing the disposal. Grant offered to drive her to Darcy's and Rebecca accepted gratefully. Brandy and York went along.

Rebecca smiled at Brandy, who chose a center seat this time. "Darcy has a huge fenced backyard where you can play with York while your dad and I help Lisa carry her stuff out to the car. But I should warn you, Darcy's boys are in perpetual motion. Watch they don't love York to death."

"We saw the boys with Lisa at Ryan's ball game, didn't we, Daddy? They're all younger than me."

"Yes, sorry," Rebecca said. "Evan is six, and Liam is five. Colt and Bart, three. I think you'll like their swing set. It looks like a pirate ship. Darcy calls it their 'doting grandparent extravaganza.'"

"With climbing ropes and ladders? Cool. I guess that could be fun," Brandy said.

In less than twenty minutes, Rebecca directed Grant to a circular drive outside a sprawling older home shaded by mature pecan trees.

Lisa had obviously been waiting for them. She

ran out the door and bounded down the front steps. Rebecca was barely out of the SUV when Lisa engulfed her in a neck-strangling hug, still babbling unintelligible apologies.

"Lisa, everything's going to be okay." It took several tries, but Rebecca managed to pry her daughter's arms loose. She couldn't help noticing that the girl looked more vulnerable now than she had before. *Jack caused this. He had no right. No right at all to scare her this badly.*

"I bet you don't remember me. I'm Brandy Lane. This is my schnauzer, York." Brandy announced her presence to Lisa. "My dad won't let that man hurt you. He flies jet planes and shoots bad guys. Pow!" Brandy emphasized descriptively, and so loudly York flattened his belly against the concrete.

Grant placed one hand on Brandy's shoulder to settle her, then extended the other to Lisa. "We didn't really get to meet the other day at my house. I'm Grant Lane, Ryan and Brandy's dad. And for the record, I no longer shoot anything. If it comes to that, which I hope it won't, San Antonio has a very able police force. I won't let anything bad happen to your mom, you or Jordan."

Before Grant finished speaking, they were joined by a blond woman a few years younger than Rebecca. "You look capable," she said, giving Grant the once-over. "I'm Darcy Blackburn. I have tea and juice, if you want to stop inside for a bit."

Rebecca kissed her friend's cheek. "Thanks,

Darce, but we left Ryan and Jordan tearing my sink apart. We'll probably load Lisa's things and be on our way. And thanks again for giving her a place to stay. Where are the boys? I told Brandy about their swing set. I thought they could show it to her while we pack the car."

"Um, the boys are spending the day with Kevin."

"You're kidding." Rebecca gaped at Darcy. "You let them go with Kevin and what's-her-name—Missy, Mitzi?"

"Mitzi. She's out of the picture. You and I haven't had a chance to talk at work. If you can believe it, Kevin sold his boat. A few weeks ago, he moved in with his folks, and now he's laying tile for his dad's construction firm. My last night off I had dinner at the Blackburns', without the boys. Kevin and I talked, and he's phoned every day since. He swears he woke up one morning and didn't like the man he saw in the mirror." Darcy met Rebecca's disbelieving gaze. "He seems genuinely changed. But I'll see how he does with the boys. I'm not committing to any more at the moment. He says he's okay with that."

Rebecca continued to stare blankly at her friend. "I can't believe you didn't tell me any of this. We could've found five minutes."

"You were preoccupied." Darcy's eyes cut to Grant, then to Lisa.

"You're right. I'm sorry. I'm beginning to realize how much my busyness has been affecting the people I care about. I'm going to be making some changes, too. But I need Lisa home. It's where she belongs. I'm sorry, Darcy, if that means you're short a sitter."

Darcy led everyone to her front door before she answered. "Hearing what's been going on, I couldn't agree more that Lisa needs to be with you. The minute she told me about her computer search, I had her do what Ryan suggested, cancel her e-mail address and Internet account. Then I made her call you."

Rebecca hugged the taller woman.

"Anyway, to ease your mind, last night I had a candidate out of the last batch of sitters I interviewed come over. She and the boys got on famously. So, we're set. Now tell me what you're going to do about Jack."

Brandy spoke up. "They need to come live with us. They'll be safe at our house."

Rebecca smiled at the girl. "You're sweet to want to protect us, but I have a policewoman friend keeping tabs on Jack. Sue phones me with updates regularly, and she said she'd call before his release."

"Mama, what did he do to be sent to prison for such a long time? He said in his e-mails that you and your cop friend framed him."

Everyone in the room turned to Rebecca, but Grant held up a hand. "Brandy, honey," he quickly interjected. "York acts like he needs a tree. Perhaps Darcy will be kind enough to show you to her backyard. You can check out that cool swing set Rebecca told you about. See if it's something you'd like in our yard."

Brandy looked as if she might refuse, but York whined and pawed at the door. "He does have to go out. I thought you were trying to get rid of me, Daddy."

Grant's guilty expression told the others Brandy had guessed right.

Darcy rushed Brandy and the dog down the long hall to her back porch.

Rebecca was grateful for the break. She took a moment to compose her thoughts. "Lisa, your dad and I split up before he went to prison. I promise you I had nothing to do with that. We grew up together. Looking back, I'm pretty sure his dad was abusive but no one ever talked about it. I loved the boy I married. We both had big hopes, even though we had no money. And he never made plans for what we'd do once we were on our own. Oh, it's so hard to talk about. He was never able to keep a job. I guess he lost sight of his dream. He changed, and his temper got worse and worse. I tried to leave and he harassed me. Sue loaned me money to disappear with you when I was pregnant with Jordan."

Grant, who was aware of how much Rebecca wasn't telling her daughter, set a bracing hand on her shoulder.

Lisa slumped. "He sounded nice on his blog, and even when we first e-mailed privately. He said he set up the blog to find his family. I couldn't believe it when he turned nasty. Like I told you, Mom, he accused you of awful things, and called you such horrid names. He even said Jordan's probably not his son." Lisa's worried eyes begged her mother for the truth.

"We should start carrying your belongings to the car, Lisa." Rebecca ran a shaky hand through her hair. "Jordan *is* Jack's son. Honey, I wish for your sake and Jordan's that your father could've been a different man. I hope you'll understand that I had to leave him."

Lisa hugged her mother. "I love you. And I've heard enough, Mom. I'm ready to go home."

"What did I miss?" Brandy asked, brushing past Darcy, who couldn't stall the girl any longer.

"Nothing," Grant and Lisa said in unison. They exchanged surprised glances that morphed into chuckles. Grant sobered first. "Brandy, you're back in time to help Lisa take her clothes to the SUV. How was the swing set? You didn't spend much time trying it out."

"It would have been cool when I was a kid, but in six months I'll be twelve. I want my ears pierced, remember."

Grant seemed at such a loss for words, Rebecca couldn't help but laugh.

Lisa had reached the first landing of the curved staircase. Peering over the rail, she commiserated with the younger girl. "I was last of my friends to get my ears pierced, too. Mom and I had ours done together when I was thirteen. She splurged and bought me gold studs for my birthday. I still have them. If it's okay with your dad, I'll let you use them."

"Can I, Daddy? Please, please?"

Grant visibly wavered. Rebecca squeezed his arm. "Don't forget what you told me, Grant. Loosen the reins."

"I remember. You, all of you," he said, "are beautiful with or without jewelry."

"Okay," Darcy said, "forget what I said in the past, Rebecca. This man's a keeper."

"I'm starting to realize that myself," Rebecca murmured, as she smiled up at Grant.

"Hooray!" Brandy shouted. "Maybe now you guys can get married."

Noticing the way Lisa tensed, Rebecca ducked out from under Grant's arm, and ran lightly up the stairs. "Brandy, you're such a tease. I know you really want my macaroni salad recipe. Hey, the boys will probably wonder what's keeping us. Lisa, let's you and I assemble your first few loads." She led her daughter away to get started.

Brandy slid her hand into Grant's. "Daddy, I wasn't teasing. I want to learn how to cook, but I want more than that, too."

"Shh, honey. I know you do. Will you hold tight to York as we carry stuff out to the car? We don't want him escaping in a strange neighborhood."

"But why can't they move into our house? You said you're going to keep them safe. How can you if they live at Rebecca's?"

"Brandy, I know you've decided Rebecca should be your stepmother. But right now she has a lot going on in her life. I'm going to talk to her, but it's only between the two of us. No one else."

"Come on, York." The child heaved a tragic sigh.

Darcy stood in the entryway taking it all in. "Would juice and chocolate chip-cookies help, Brandy?"

"I guess so." Grant smiled as he watched his daughter skip after Darcy.

THEY WERE in the SUV, headed back to Rebecca's when Brandy produced the recipe card Darcy had given her. "Darcy made the yummiest cookies I ever ate. She wrote her special recipe out for me so Rebecca can bake them when she moves in with us."

Lisa snatched the card. "Huh! This is the recipe printed on every chocolate-chip package. Did Darcy tell you it was a secret?"

Brandy yanked the recipe back. "Special, not secret. They were yummy."

"Then *you* bake them. My mom's not moving," Lisa said. "Tell her, Mom. We have a nice home."

"Kids, kids," Grant admonished. "Can you please get along for ten more minutes?"

The girls traded barbed glances, but didn't speak.

Grant soon pulled into Rebecca's driveway. Ryan and Jordan barreled out of the side door. "The disposal is in and working," Ryan announced proudly before his dad or the others climbed from the SUV.

"Yep, it gobbled everything we fed it," Jordan said, grinning broadly as he opened his mom's door.

"That's fantastic, boys," she said. "I thought it would take a lot longer to install."

"Hey, guys." Grant waved them over. "Give us a hand hauling Lisa's stuff in, please."

"We're pooped," Jordan said. "Let her carry it. She carted it to Darcy's by herself."

Ryan nudged the younger boy. "I helped her move to Darcy's, remember?"

"Scram, all of you." Rebecca shooed them away. "I don't want to listen to any more bickering. Grant and I can move it alone. It's not that big a deal."

"Why?" Lisa demanded. "So you two can make out?"

"Okay, that's it! I've been more than patient because there was a lot you and Jordan didn't know. Now you do, so listen up. Grant and I don't need chaperones. If we want to kiss each other, we will." As if to underscore her point, Rebecca latched on to the front of Grant's shirt and kissed him soundly.

"I told you so!" Brandy poked Lisa's ribs. "They're in love, and gonna get maarried!" She sang off-key and danced around the older girl.

"No one said that," Rebecca said, pulling back.

Grant scowled at their offspring. "I'd planned to wait until we had the SUV unloaded so we could go inside for a group talk. But you're all pushing, so I'll say it now. I like Rebecca, and I want to keep seeing her. The only permission I need is hers."

"Mother!" Lisa continued to balk.

"Permission granted," Rebecca said, her eyes on Grant.

"But I want you to get married," Brandy wailed.

Grant hushed her. "We may decide that's what we want to do. If that happens, I promise, we'll sit down with you kids before we book a church. All four of you. Is that clear?"

Four heads nodded. Grant grinned sheepishly before draping an arm around Rebecca's shoulders again. "You're the only one allowed to object at this stage," he said, planting kisses along the edge of her ear.

"No objections so far," she murmured, stretching to give him access to her neck.

"I'm glad, Becca." He hugged her tightly.

"What about Lisa e-mailing our dad? And all the other junk she said when she phoned?" Jordan asked, pulling Grant and Rebecca back to reality.

Rebecca flattened her palm on Grant's chest. "Would you and Ryan mind helping Lisa unload her things? Brandy can take York to his water dish in the laundry room. I need ten minutes in private with my kids first."

Grant opened the back of the SUV and started passing bags to Ryan.

Rebecca hustled her two into her bedroom and shut the door. "There was a time I was so afraid of your dad getting out and somehow finding us, I was nearly paralyzed and could barely function." She didn't sugarcoat her struggles, but neither did she tell them more than they needed to know. "I won't pretend I don't wish Lisa had never made contact with Jack. But he's in Oregon and we're in Texas."

Lisa's face turned pasty white. "He said he has friends here, and he says he's going to come find us when he gets out. Maybe we *should* move in with Mr. Lane for a while." Lisa's lips trembled. "Daddy *hates* you, Mom."

"He has no reason to hate me, honey. I'll call Sue. She said once that there's always a kind of mustering-out meeting in the warden's office the day a prisoner's released. If I explain about Jack's blog and Web site, and what he wrote in e-mails to you, she may influence the terms of his release. And even if she can't, I should have grounds to file a re-straining order here in San Antonio."

"Okay." Lisa looked slightly reassured. Jordan, too. "Then you're not in a huge rush to marry Mr. Lane?" Lisa added.

"I care about Grant very much. I'm just not ready to thrust his family into the middle of my problems if I can take care of them myself."

Jordan, who'd been sitting on the floor, jumped up and threw his arms around his mother. "I love you, Mom. And I know you're tough. But Grant's bigger. He's got money, too. More than us. At school in economics class, Ms. Greenbaum said money equals power."

"Jordan!" Rebecca unlooped his arms from around her neck. She gripped his hands, but included both kids in her stern gaze. "Grant's money has nothing to do with my feelings for him. Zero. Are we clear?" The two nodded mutely and Rebecca strode to the door. "We shouldn't keep our guests waiting any longer. And Lisa has her things to put away." She opened the door and let Lisa and Jordan file out first.

The TV blared. Grant sprang to his feet the minute Rebecca and kids walked in. "Is everything all right?" he asked, studying first one face then the others.

"Fine," Rebecca said. "Tonight I'm going to phone Sue Crenshaw. If she can't get his sentence extended, she'll have the exact date of his release. We'll put a big black X on our calendar. The kids and I will be extra careful for a week or two thereafter. I imagine he'll be busy trying to get a job, anyway."

Ryan muted the TV. "What about his threats?"

"Mom thinks it's all talk," Lisa said, planting herself on the arm of the couch nearest Ryan.

Grant chewed the inside of his mouth. "I'd like the date when you get it from your friend, too, Becca. I'd feel better hiring some muscle to stick with you for a month or so, and someone to keep an eye on the house when you're out."

"Hire muscle? Are you kidding me?"

"Okay, call them bodyguards. A lot of ex-military go into that business. I'm sure I can find a reliable firm in San Antonio."

Rebecca tried, but couldn't contain her laughter. "Sorry. Grant, I'm sure bodyguards cost the earth. Besides, it's all too Tony Soprano."

He stepped closer to her and gently held her face in his hands. "I love you. I would pay any amount of money to keep you and Jordan and Lisa safe from harm. If I drained my savings, I could get a job with a military contractor training flyers. Money's nice, but it's worth nothing if you can't spend it on the people you love."

Tears welled in Rebecca's eyes. The kids, even the boys, were impressed with Grant's speech. "Mom," Lisa whispered shakily, "that offer came from his heart. You need to pay attention. You've always taken care of us. Mr. Lane wants to help."

"Grant," Jordan growled at his sister. "He said we can call him Grant."

Rebecca lifted her hands and circled Grant's wrists. She could feel the steady beat of his pulse, and, even through a sheen of tears, saw the true depth of love and caring in his eyes.

In a soft voice she asked, "How would all of you feel about Lisa and Jordan calling Grant…Dad?"

It took a few moments for the kids and Grant to process what Rebecca had said. Grant seized on it first. He picked her up and let out a happy whoop. The kids began giving each other high fives. Even York got into the act, barking and chasing his stubby tail.

Eventually, the nervous uneasiness that accompanied major change set in. This time the kids reacted to the silence. They shuffled their seating, dividing themselves along family lines. Lisa scraped at her peeling pink fingernail polish, but she ventured to ask the question that was on everyone's minds. "Does that mean he, Mr. Lane, uh, Grant, will adopt Jordan and me?"

Lacing his fingers with Rebecca's, Grant sat himself and Rebecca down in the too-small space between the groups of kids. "This is as good a time as any to hash this out. Let me say I would be honored and pleased to be your dad. Now let's hear from you guys. What are you thinking?"

Rebecca paused to wipe her eyes on her sleeve before she spoke. "I think it has to be the kids' decision. Not only Lisa and Jordan, but Ryan and Brandy need a say."

Brandy held York on her lap. She burrowed in next to her brother. Where she'd been exuberant before, it was clear she was going to let Ryan take the lead.

He rotated a shoulder casually. "I graduate at the end of May. By September I'll be at college. Coach thinks I might get a baseball scholarship to A & M University. Or I could try Baylor. Either way I'll live on campus. I guess I'm trying to say it doesn't affect me as much as the rest of you."

"It might involve your inheritance," Rebecca put in quietly, glancing at Grant. "We could sign a pre-nuptial agreement excluding me and my kids."

"That's not going to happen. You'll be my wife

and I'm going to provide for you and our family. At our age, Becca, it'll be a long time before our kids inherit. Bright as they all are, I'm counting on them out-earning their old man."

"If you adopted us, does that mean you'll pay college tuition for Lisa and me, too? And Mom can quit work?" Jordan asked.

"Jordan," Rebecca said, sitting forward and frowning at her son. "I earned my beauty license, and I'm proud of that. I can work, and I plan to."

"Your second job, then. You should get to quit that. Their house is bigger than ours, and there's more people to feed and more laundry to do," Jordan said stubbornly.

Brandy kicked his knee. "They're getting married. Rebecca's not coming to our house to be a cook or housekeeper. She's gonna be a regular mother, Jordan."

Grant and Rebecca traded wry grins at that exchange. "Brandy, honey," Rebecca said, "I want to contribute to the family in any way I can. I'm sure I'll do my share of cooking and cleaning—and so will your dad. Jordan, I appreciate your wanting to look out for my welfare. You've been the man of our family, and you've handled the responsibility beautifully. Won't it be nice not to have to do that anymore? You'll be able to just be a kid."

He considered the idea a minute, then he grinned and a smile lit his ocean-colored eyes that were so like his mother's.

"How soon will all this happen?" Ryan asked. "I mean, you guys obviously need to move into our house ASAP, with the threats Mr. Geroux made to Lisa. I just wonder how much time Lisa and I will have to explain to kids at school how we went from 'dating' to being brother and sister."

Lisa reached up from where she sat and lightly smacked Ryan's leg. "I know what you're really worried about. Emily Sikes and Brooke Gilroy will be all over you. Oh, and Courtney Wilson. She'll be at your locker constantly." Lisa's laugh was almost diabolical. Ryan groaned and let his head roll back on his shoulders.

"When is the wedding?" Brandy asked. "Daddy, you have to buy Rebecca a ring. And, Lisa, you and I can get new dresses. Long, fancy ones. Your mom needs a beautiful dress, too. Lacy and white."

Grant whistled shrilly. "Hold on. Let's not go too quickly. Rebecca already told me she doesn't want diamonds." He paused and turned to look at her. "I want to buy you a ring, though. How do you feel about sapphires or emeralds? Our backyard is a nice place to hold a ceremony. A simple, casual ceremony," he said, dragging Rebecca's hand to his lips to kiss her knuckles. "I would like a minister. That's my only request. I want us to repeat the traditional vows that so many have used before us."

"Oh, Grant, you're going to make me cry again. This is all so overwhelming. Can we get matching bands?" She dragged in a deep breath and probably would have said more, but the phone rang.

"Want me to get it?" Lisa asked, uncrossing her legs.

"Stay here. I'll grab it," Rebecca said, standing up from the couch. She moved to the kitchen door and lifted the receiver with a cheery hello.

In the living room, the kids had begun to discuss aspects of the wedding. But Grant noticed Rebecca sag against the door frame, and waved the kids quiet.

He quickly joined her in the kitchen.

"Sue, what's going on?" Her voice shook.

Rebecca glanced up, met Grant's eyes, and at once reached out, clutching his arm.

"I am…shocked to say the least," she said. "Maybe even floored. On the other hand, I could say it's not really a surprise, tragic as it is."

Leaning her icy cheek against Grant's hand, Rebecca gave Sue Crenshaw the details of Lisa's recent Internet encounter with her dad.

"Sue, I need to talk to the kids about this." Her eyes were wide and suddenly brimming with tears. "I'll have to call you back. You won't know any more until tomorrow, right? Okay, noon tomorrow, after the bail hearing. They won't grant bail, will they? I didn't think so. This was hardly the news I expected, but I can't thank you enough for keeping me in the loop." She hung up, and didn't argue when Grant led her back to the couch.

The kids waited. It was obvious they'd heard

enough of the conversation to be worried. In fact, as Rebecca sat gathering her wits, the four young people moved closer together and joined hands. York was the only one unaffected.

"Okay, it's hard knowing where to start," Rebecca said, sitting straight, gripping her knees to steady her hands. "That was Sue Crenshaw. She said Jack..." Pausing, Rebecca licked her lips. "Jack and two other inmates broke out of prison this morning."

"What?" The kids' shouting woke York. He scrambled up and barked loudly. Brandy gathered him close. Ryan slipped an arm around his sister and their pet.

"It's true. They overpowered a guard and somehow got past the fence. But it's okay now. All three were apprehended about an hour ago. Sue received the official notice from her supervisor."

"You mentioned a bail hearing," Grant prompted.

"Lisa, Jordan, I don't know how to tell you this. I have such mixed emotions myself. I can't believe Jack would be so stupid when he was this close to getting out anyway. The guard they overpowered died. Your father, and the men he was with, will face capital murder charges."

Lisa looked stricken. "Will—will he get the death penalty? I don't mind knowing he'll be locked up forever, but..." Her eyes filled.

Grant leaned over and wiped a tear off her pale cheek. "If you'd like, Lisa, we can take the money I was going to use for bodyguards, and get your dad a good lawyer. Someone willing to fight to get your father a life sentence."

"You'd do that?" Lisa exclaimed.

Grant nodded.

Jordan simply got up and hugged Grant tightly.

Rebecca let her tears fall unabashedly.

"I loved you already," she said quietly. "What you're offering to do is beyond selfless. It puts you at the opposite end of the spectrum from the man you're willing to assist. I told Darcy you were a good man, but I've changed my mind, Grant. You're a great man."

Grant turned several shades of red, and tried to make light of the whole thing. No one would let him. But it was Brandy who put it best. "When we moved to San Antonio I prayed I'd get a mother and a puppy. I'm about the luckiest girl in the world, 'cause both wishes came true. Plus, I got a sister and another brother. I figure my home in Texas is pretty much perfect."

After the teasing petered out, as the teens settled to watch TV and Rebecca and Grant snuggled together on the sofa, Brandy's sentiment was echoed throughout the roomful of people about to become family.

* * * * *

Triple Trouble
by
Lois Faye Dyer

Nicholas Fortune closed the financial data file on his computer and stretched. Yawning, he pushed his chair away from his desk and stood. His office was on the top floor of the building housing the Fortune Foundation, and outside the big corner windows, the Texas night was moonless, the sky a black dome spangled with the faint glitter of stars.

"Hell of a lot different from L.A.," he mused aloud, his gaze tracing the moving lights of an airplane far above. The view from the window in his last office in a downtown Los Angeles high rise too often had been blurred with smog that usually blotted out the stars. No, Red Rock, Texas, was more than just a few thousand miles from California—it was a whole world away.

All in all, he thought as he gazed into the darkness, he was glad he'd moved here a month ago. He'd grown tired of his job as a financial analyst for the Kline Corporation in L.A. and needed new challenges—working for the family foundation allowed him time to contemplate his next career move. And a nice side benefit was that he got to spend more time with his brother, Darr.

With the exception of the hum of a janitor's vacuum in the hallway outside, the building around him was as silent as the street below. Nicholas turned away from the window and returned to his desk to slide his laptop into its leather carrying case. He was just shrugging into his jacket when his cell phone rang.

He glanced at his watch. The fluorescent dials read eleven-fifteen. He didn't recognize the number and ordinarily would have let the call go to voice mail, but for some reason he thumbed the On button. "Hello?"

"Mr. Fortune? Nicholas Fortune?"

He didn't recognize the male voice. "Yes."

"Ah, excellent." Relief echoed in the man's voice. "I'm sorry to call so late, but I've been trying to locate you for three days and my assistant just found this number. My name is Andrew Sanchez. I'm an attorney for the estate of Stan Kennedy."

Nicholas froze, his fingers tightening on the slim black cell phone. "The *estate* of Stan Kennedy? Did something happen to Stan?"

"I'm sorry to be the bearer of unfortunate news." The caller's voice held regret. "Mr. Kennedy and his wife were killed in a car accident three days ago."

Shock kept Nicholas mute.

"Mr. Fortune?"

"Yeah." Nicholas managed to force words past the thick emotion clogging his throat. "Yeah, I'm here."

"It's my understanding you and Mr. Kennedy were quite close?"

"We were college roommates. I haven't seen Stan in a year or so, but we keep in touch—*kept* in touch by phone and e-mail." *Like brothers,* Nicholas thought. "We were close as brothers in college."

"I see. Well, Mr. Fortune, that probably explains why he named you guardian of his children. The little girls are currently safe and in the care of a foster mother, but the caseworker is anxious to transfer custody to you. The sooner they're in a stable environment the better."

"Whoa, wait a minute." Nicholas shook his head to clear it, convinced he hadn't heard the attorney correctly. "Stan left *me* in charge of his kids?"

"Yes, that's correct." The attorney paused. "You didn't know?"

Nicholas tried to remember exactly what Stan had told him about his will. They'd both agreed to take care of business for the other if anything happened to them. He'd been Stan's best man at his wedding to Amy and he definitely remembered Stan asking him to look after his bride should anything happen. Even though their conversation had taken place while emptying a magnum of champagne, Nicholas knew his word was important to Stan and he hadn't given it lightly.

But *babies?* And not just one—*three.*

"The triplets weren't born when we made a pact to look after each other's estate, should anything ever happen," he told the attorney. *And neither of us thought he and Amy wouldn't live to raise their daughters.* "But I promised Stan I'd take care of his family if he couldn't."

"Excellent." The attorney's voice was full of relief. "Can I expect you at my office tomorrow, then?"

"Tomorrow?" Nick repeated, his voice rough with shock.

"I know it's extremely short notice," Sanchez said apologetically. "But as I said, the caseworker is very concerned that the babies be settled in a permanent situation as soon as possible."

"Uh, yeah, I suppose that makes sense," Nick said. He thrust his fingers through his hair and tried to focus on the calendar that lay open on his desktop. "I've got a meeting I can't cancel in the morning, but I'll catch the first flight out after lunch." Nicholas jotted down the address in Amarillo and hung up. It was several moments before he realized he was sitting on the edge of his desk, staring at the silent phone, still open in his hand.

Grief washed over him, erasing the cold, numbing shock that had struck with the news. He couldn't believe Stan and Amy were gone. The couple met life with a zest few of their friends could match. It was impossible to get his head around the fact that all their vibrant energy had been snuffed out.

He scrubbed his hand down his face and his fingers came away damp.

He sucked in a deep breath and stood. He didn't have time to mourn Stan and Amy. Their deaths had left their three little girls vulnerable, without the protection of parents. Though how the hell Stan and Amy had ever decided he was the best choice to act as substitute dad for the triplets, Nicholas couldn't begin to guess.

In all his thirty-seven years, he'd never spent any length of time around a baby. He had four brothers but no wife, no fiancée or sister, and his mom had died two years ago. The only permanent female in his immediate family was Barbara, the woman his brother Darr had fallen in love with a month earlier. Barbara was pregnant. Did that mean she knew about babies?

Nick hadn't a clue. And for a guy who spent his life dealing with the predictability of numbers, in his career as a financial analyst, being clueless didn't sit well.

But he had no choice.

Despite being totally unqualified for the job, he was flying to Amarillo tomorrow.

And bringing home three babies.

He didn't know a damn thing about kids. Especially not little girls.

He was going to have to learn fast….

Charlene London walked quickly along the Red Rock Airport concourse, nearly running as she hurried to the gate. The flight to Amarillo was already boarding and only a few stragglers like herself waited to be checked through.

Fortunately, the uniformed airline attendant was efficient, and a moment later, Charlene joined the short queue of passengers waiting to board.

For the first time in the last hour, she drew a deep breath and relaxed. The last three weeks had been hectic and difficult. Breaking up with her fiancé after three years had been hard, but quitting her job, packing her apartment and putting everything in storage had been draining. She'd purposely pared her luggage down to a few bags, since she'd be living with her mother in a condo in Amarillo while she looked for a job and an apartment.

And a new life, she told herself. She was determined to put her failed relationship with Barry behind her and get on with her career.

She sipped her latte, mentally updating her résumé while the line moved slowly forward. They entered the plane and her eyes widened at the packed cabin and aisle, still thronged with passengers finding seats and stowing bags in the overhead compartments.

Thank goodness I used my frequent flyer miles to upgrade to first class. She glanced at her ticket and scanned the numbers above the seats, pausing as she found hers.

"Excuse me."

The man rose and stepped into the aisle to let her move past him to reach the window seat.

He smelled wonderful. Charlene didn't recognize

the scent, but it was subtle and clean. Probably incredibly expensive. *And thank goodness he isn't wearing the same cologne as Barry,* she thought with a rush of relief.

She was trying to get away from Barry—and didn't need or want any reminder of her ex-boyfriend. Or fiancé. Or whatever the appropriate term was for the man you'd dated for three whole years, thinking he was the man you'd marry, until you'd discovered that he was…not the man you'd thought he was at all.

Very disheartening.

"Can I put that up for you?"

The deep male voice rumbled, yanking Charlene from her reverie.

"What?" She realized he was holding out his hand, the expression on his very handsome face expectant. He lifted a brow, glanced significantly at her carry-on, then at her. "Oh, yes. Thank you."

He swung the bag up with ease while she slipped into the window seat. She focused on latching her seat belt, stowing her purse under the seat and settling in. It wasn't until the plane backed away from the gate to taxi toward the runaway that she really looked at the man beside her.

He was staring at the inflight magazine but Charlene had the distinct impression he wasn't reading. In profile, his face was all angles with high cheekbones, chiseled lips and a strong jawline. His dark brown hair was short, just shy of a buzz cut, and from her side view, his eyelashes were amazingly long and thick. She wondered idly what color his eyes were.

She didn't wonder long. He glanced up, his gaze meeting hers.

Brown. His eyes were brown. *The kind of eyes a woman could lose herself in,* she thought hazily.

His eyes darkened, lashes half lowering as he studied her.

Charlene's breath caught at the male interest he didn't bother to hide. Her skin heated, her nipples peaking beneath the soft lace of her bra.

Stunned at the depth of her reaction, she couldn't pull her gaze from his.

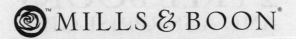

2 FREE BOOKS
AND A SURPRISE GIFT

We would like to take this opportunity to thank you for reading this Mills & Boon® book by offering you the chance to take TWO more specially selected books from the Special Moments™ series absolutely FREE! We're also making this offer to introduce you to the benefits of the Mills & Boon® Book Club™—

- **FREE home delivery**
- **FREE gifts and competitions**
- **FREE monthly Newsletter**
- **Exclusive Mills & Boon Book Club offers**
- **Books available before they're in the shops**

Accepting these FREE books and gift places you under no obligation to buy, you may cancel at any time, even after receiving your free books. Simply complete your details below and return the entire page to the address below. You don't even need a stamp!

YES Please send me 2 free Special Moments books and a surprise gift. I understand that unless you hear from me, I will receive 5 superb new stories every month, including a 2-in-1 book priced at £4.99 and three single books priced at £3.19 each, postage and packing free. I am under no obligation to purchase any books and may cancel my subscription at any time. The free books and gift will be mine to keep in any case.

Ms/Mrs/Miss/Mr _____ Initials _____

_____

Surname _____

Address _____

_____

_____ Postcode _____

Send this whole page to: Mills & Boon Book Club, Free Book Offer, FREEPOST NAT 10298, Richmond, TW9 1BR